The Discovery
of America

The Discovery of America

and Other Tales of

Terror and Self-Exploration

Stories by ALVIN GREENBERG

LOUISIANA STATE UNIVERSITY PRESS
Baton Rouge and London 1980

Copyright © 1980 by Alvin Greenberg
All rights reserved
Manufactured in the United States of America

Design: Albert Crochet
Typeface: VIP Souvenir
Composition: LSU Press
Printing and binding: Thomson-Shore, Inc.

Some of the stories in this volume appeared originally in
*New American Review; Antioch Review; Fiction International;
Massachusetts Review; New Letters; Remington Review;*
and *Tri-Quarterly*.

LIBRARY OF CONGRESS CATALOGING IN PUBLICATION DATA
Greenberg, Alvin.
    The discovery of America and other tales of terror
and self-exploration.

    I. Title.
PZ4.G7984Di   [PS3557.R377]   813'.5'4   79–13068
ISBN 0–8071–0591–0

To the memory of Wendy Parrish

"I . . . suddenly realize where I am, I
am in your story."

Contents

The Discovery
of America

The Origins of Life

When vacation time comes and others pack up, with family or friends, for Miami Beach or Paris, Grand Canyon or Glacier National Park, Honolulu or Penobscott Bay, I am left to head off all alone for one of the great rain forests of the world: Ceylon, Malaysia, West Africa, the Amazon or Orinoco basins. The moment the office shuts down, I leave for the airport, already packed, my ticket paid for, my passport and immunization record up to date. The following morning I land in Colombo and immediately catch the train to Kandy, high up in the central mountains. There I spend the night at a government tourist bungalow and the following day take the bus part way back down the mountains, into one of the high, rain-soaked valleys on the western slope. An hour out of Kandy the asphalt road gives way to dirt. The monsoon is early this year; another couple of days and the road will perhaps become impassable. I may be forced to overstay my time, or be brought out by bullock cart, but I am indifferent to such matters. I am almost there. By midafternoon, when we reach the small village at the roadhead, it is raining heavily. The bus stops in front of a coffee shop, but I have to stand in the rain and mud and wait for the driver to hand down my suitcase from the roof before I can go inside. The tiny shop is crowded at this hour and I am invited to share a table with three villagers, two of whom speak English. One of them agrees to take me into his home for the night and even insists on carrying my suitcase. We walk slowly through the warm, heavy rain to his hut at the edge of the forest. His wife smiles shyly when she serves us dinner, but does not speak. We

1

go to sleep as soon as it is dark but I awake later in the night, when the rain has stopped, and go outside in the dark. Except for the dripping from the trees, all is silent, and there are no stars to be seen.

In the morning the man, who knows where there is an abandoned hut, takes me into the forest. He still insists on carrying my suitcase. We follow a narrow, muddy footpath around the side of a hill for several miles, but when we arrive we find the hut is occupied by two old women and a large number of children. He argues with them at some length but it is obvious that they will not leave. At last he gives up and we return to his home. We eat, nap, and, as the afternoon passes, sit in the doorway and watch the rain begin again. At last he suggests that I remain in his home. With little effort we agree on a reasonable price for my room and board. I am free to spend my days in the forest or where I will. There are two small children, twins I believe, whom I have not seen previously. Like the wife, they do not speak but smile shyly whenever they see me. The man is around the house most of the time. I am in the forest. In the evenings, when I return, we talk softly, mostly about the varieties of plant and animal life in the forest. The bus comes irregularly. The days pass. Late each afternoon the rain begins, usually while I am still in the forest. We eat lightly, retire as soon as it is dark. Because the bus cannot get through I leave a day late, but have no trouble making connections for the return flight.

At home I hear my co-workers asking each other, "How was it?" From the answers they exchange I understand that they mean, was Stockholm as interesting as Rome? was the weather nice? did your wife and kids have a good time? did you buy souvenirs? eat well? When at last they turn to me, they ask, "What was it like?" What I understand them to mean is, What was it like?

Well, I try to tell them, it's very interesting. But that isn't enough. They want to know what it's *like*, what it's *really* like, in the most concrete terms I can summon up. So I do the best I can, though it isn't what interests me. I name several varieties each of tropical birds and exotic flowering plants, although the truth is I can no longer distinguish among them myself. I speak of the timing of the monsoons, of hundreds of inches of rainfall per year, of the leaching of volcanic soils. All this data falls on deaf ears. I say that it's hot (*unbearably* hot, I add, which meets at last with considerable approval), humid, dark, smelly, mosquito-filled. . . . But none of that suffices, of course; it only provokes a further question: Why do you go there? They do not ask, of each other, why do you go to Austria (old-world flavor) or Guadalajara (good shopping) or California (sun, sea, sex), but, only of me, why do you go *there*? Did you buy anything? No (not in the sense intended). Did you take any pictures? No (true). Meet anybody interesting? No (a palpable lie). Have a nice time? No (no!). Then why do you *go* there? I shrug my shoulders, implying ignorance of my own motives—a half truth, the best I can do till more is known, but the other half of the truth is not likely to satisfy them, they want to know *why* I go there, the real reason, and a solid, self-confessed ignorance meets their demand far better than a vaporous, half-formed supposition.

When I retire into my office I am, once more, unhappy with the way this postvacation interview has gone. I don't ask *them* why they go to Las Vegas or the White Mountains, though sometimes they supply the answer without the question: I like excitement, I like to soak up the sun, I found a bargain-priced tour, I've never lived where there weren't mountains before. And sometimes, too, as the sun moves north through Pisces, sign of the vacationer, they approach with greater candor to say, I don't care where I go, I've just got to get away. But of course they cannot simply get away, they have to get away to somewhere in particular, and to pursue the matter, one ought to ask them, why Edinburgh instead of Taos, Anchorage instead of Cumberland Gap? And so come at least a little closer. But that is not the direction I am interested in going, not even the direction I take with my own going. I only want to go to the rain forest. I want to go *back* to the rain forest.

ii

Marsha, who is afraid of bugs, refuses to accompany me into the rain forest. After I returned from my first journey (Burma) she kept me up

all night playing country music ballads, each of them about a man
who wanted to break out, hit the road, and head west. Cowboys,
truck drivers, linemen, ex-soldiers, and just plain working stiffs, they
all had the same idea: movin' on. I was well aware of the theme.
Even without her able commentary it had the twang of truth to it.
Amplified guitar sounds only served to make its long and humorless
history all the more resonant. But Burma, I had to point out, was in
what was usually considered the East. I was unable, at the time, to
defend myself against the charge of quibbling. Nonetheless, by dawn
I had begun to lay out, for myself at least, some of the pieces of a
concept of going back. By the next year, the next vacation (alone of
course), the next rain forest (the Amazon), I had even begun to fit a
few of those pieces together: the corners and straight edges, though
the vast interior was dark and humid and shapeless still.

Meanwhile, August dry spells burn the lawns brown and shrivel
crops. The newspapers report all-time lows in the reservoirs, and the
city council debates restrictions on water usage. Forest fires rage in
the hills above Los Angeles. Airconditioners fall victim to inadequate
power supplies. Our weekends we spend at the beach, though we
approach the water's edge only to build sand castles or to watch the
tide go out. On Saturday nights we see *Lawrence of Arabia* with
great regularity, or stay up late watching reruns of French Foreign
Legion films on TV. I return from South America to find that Marsha,
in my absence, has been to visit the Mojave and the Great Salt Lake.
She, who has always been a student of fine literature (*Green Man-
sions! Heart of Darkness!*), is suddenly reading *Desert Ecology, A
Natural History of the Southwest, Seven Pillars of Wisdom, Adven-
tures in the Gobi*. A book on *Desert Warfare* by an Israeli general
graces the coffee table; on her nightstand is the latest issue of *National
Geographic*, opened to a lavishly illustrated article on Bedouin tribal
life. At dinner, the evening after my return from the Congo, she
serves a cactus salad she has learned to make on her recent trip to
Mexico. It is good, but it is also too much.

"Marsha," I say. I have demonstrated both good faith and good appetite by eating every bit of my salad. "Marsha, I do not wish to engage in desert warfare with you."

Finishing her own salad, she smiles, a smile that antedates her new readings by many years and yet would lead me, should she choose to use it for such an end, into the most barren of deserts, places where life has not been known for centuries. The smile, however, is simply her terrain, an Israel that, inexplicably, borders my Ecuador. In it, under her benign governance, immigrants from distant climactic zones labor at unexpected trades, the desert blooms, cities rise, new families are founded and flourish, and an ancient language is resurrected, uncongenial to tourists. Nor is she incapable of defending her borders.

I get up to fetch my fish and rice casserole from the oven. Gently, with a politic seriousness and only a touch of dry humor, her voice follows me into the kitchen: "Where will you go when you run out of rain forests?"

Where indeed? Once, perhaps, rain forests denser than any that now survive covered most of the land mass of the earth. Today scientists propose the clearing and development of the Amazon basin. Tomorrow, Marsha, the bulldozer that uproots the breadfruit and lignum vitae, rips down the lianas, and sends the brightly plumaged birds screaming into the sky, may find me standing in its path, naked, flightless, and alone. Then. But it is now that I am interested in, not then, and my present steams and drips around the edges like the casserole I lift from the oven with my heavily gloved hands. I want to offer her full citizenship in this, my would-be homeland, but even *I* don't know its language yet and so can only respond with inane guidebook phrases.

"And you," I ask, as I carry the casserole to the table, "when all the deserts have been turned into fertile fields, will you want to visit Minnesota's Sand Dune State Park, where it is rumored one sand dune still remains?"

"Perhaps," she smiles. "Is that an invitation?" With one gloved hand I lift the top from the casserole. A dense cloud of steam rises.

When it clears she notices at once the strange object I have placed in the center of the casserole.

Wilted now beyond recognition, it was, I explain, a tree orchid.

"From Brazil?" she asks.

"Africa," I correct her. "No. I tried to bring some home on the plane, but they wouldn't let me take them through customs. I picked this one up at the florist shop near my office. Home grown, I suppose. I'm sorry, I didn't know cooking would make such a mess of it."

"Do you think it's safe?" she asks, stirring the casserole around a bit with the serving spoon.

"Safe?" I repeat.

"I mean," she says, "I never heard of eating orchids. Maybe when they're cooked they give off some sort of poison."

For a long time we both sit at the table and stare at the casserole. It still steams slightly. Finally Marsha gets up and goes to the kitchen and returns with an extra plate. With the serving spoon, I lift the grey and soggy orchid from the casserole and place it on the empty dish. As I lift it, however, parts crumble and fall back, and these pieces I have to pick out of the casserole one by one. When we are both satisfied that all of the flower has been removed, we settle down to watch the casserole again. Finally, just before the casserole becomes too cool to eat, we both dig in with our own utensils—the serving spoon, parts of the flower still stuck to it, having been laid aside— heap our plates full, and within minutes, have eaten all the rice and fish. This devouring of the casserole, it occurs to me, is carried out with all the speed and precision of a suicide pact.

iii

In the jungles of the Orinoco I lay me down and immediately bird watchers spring up all about me. I did not know such a thing was possible, but I have become part of a tour. At first, therefore, I do not believe they are observing me, only watching me out of the corners of their eyes, keeping track of my posture in relation to the scene, the setting. As, on the airplane, chirping happily together, they took only so much note, and no more, of the meals and the in-flight movie. The thing I like about them is their ability to ignore the ways in which they themselves are in the midst of the same setting. Here, raindrops seem to pass right through them. Mosquitoes ignore them. If sunlight were to reach this depth, would they, I wonder, cast shadows? The warbler count rises. They are, thank God, not especially interested in exotica, but here in the gloomy twilight of the forest can spot, in the gap between a wild orchid and a blue-crowned motmot, the jerky movements of your ordinary robin. From where I lie, my sticky back cooling against the soggy trunk of a fallen, rotting tree, I can hear their cries of joy. What I like about them is the way their own numbers expand, the moment you turn your back upon them, to include the most unlikely people. The TWA stewardesses, for example, the bus-boys from the Alameda Hotel, where I know they are staying, a number of native schoolchildren. They are ill-concealed and talk much too loudly, the old-timers as well as the newcomers. There is not a camera in sight, and only one pair of binoculars among them all. What I like best about them is that they want me in the living flesh.

In the evening I walk into town to have a drink on the veranda of their hotel. I take a seat next to a lovely, grey-haired woman and order a brandy from the waiter as he passes by. When he returns, I pay for the drink and turn toward this woman, who sits quietly on my left. Even under the yellow bulbs that light the veranda, her skin glows a pale white.

"Did you have a good day in the forest?" I ask her.

"Oh yes," she says, "there's so much to see. There's always so much to see." She crosses her legs and sips a frothy fruit punch from a long-stemmed glass. The mosquitoes hum and dive around us. Most of her companions have retired, or at least gone indoors.

"Do you often come to the rain forests?" I ask.

"Often?" she echoes. "No. Tomorrow we go to the mountains. Next year we're going to Australia."

"Darwin," I say, "the north coast of the Northern Territory. I haven't been there yet."

"No," she counters, "Western Australia. The Great Sandy Desert, Eighty Mile Beach. Waders and warblers, perhaps even one of the flightless species."

"Flightless species?" I inquire.

"Like the emu," she explains, "Great ugly things, but I suppose they also have to be seen."

"Have to be seen?" I echo again, while she uncrosses her legs, smoothes her skirt, and crosses them again. "But why?"

"I don't suppose," she says, looking slightly away from me, "you spend all your time in rain forests. You were, after all, on the plane that brought us here. Unless you were just coming from another rain forest."

"Another rain forest," I say, laughing. "No, no, hardly, unless you were to consider my office. . . ." I trail off. It's an interesting thought, however. Certain clearly defined levels of growth, a few well-buttressed giants, a multitude of creepers, soft carpeting, a damp atmosphere of near-familiarity.

She leans very close into the silence I have built about myself and says, "You know, you ought to try alpine meadows sometime, or even deserts."

"Well," I say, sitting abruptly forward on the edge of my chair, "perhaps there's something to what you say. However." Holding my long-empty glass between my sweaty palms I look around for the waiter. Instead, I see the faces of the bird watchers peering out at me through the heavily screened windows that look onto the veranda. Here and there fingers are poked in my direction, as if to point out some identifying characteristic. In their whispers, I assume they are discussing the pattern of my movements. When I turn to my companion again, she has risen and is standing calmly beside her chair. Standing up to face her, I explain to her that I am not yet finished with the rain forest, that I have, in fact, just begun. The waiter appears out of the darkness at the far end of the veranda, scoops up our glasses onto his tray, and retreats into the darkness again, without pausing to take a new order.

"Of course," she says, "you must be right." Then she takes my damp fingers into her own dry palm for a moment and is gone. Left to pursue my beginnings alone, I leave the veranda, follow the street that crosses in front of the hotel out beyond the edge of the town, stumble, in the dark, across the surrounding ring of fields, follow a twisting forest path for some half mile onward to where I have staked out a small tent, plunge through the mosquito netting, and topple at once onto the soggy sheets of my cot. There, in my tent, in the forest, in the night, I am trapped immediately in the heavy net of sleep. I thrash around mightily but cannot get free. In the dark I sweat profusely and utter hoarse, inarticulate cries as I flap my arms and legs wildly about. Through the webbing of the net I see the faces of the bird watchers staring at me, wide-eyed. They are pointing at various parts of my body and taking notes on my markings. They sit gently on the netting to pin down my flailing limbs. At the same time they begin to question me. What are my mating habits? Where do I build my nest? Am I a migratory species? I deny it. Ha ha, they laugh, we'll see you here next year. Oh no you won't, I squawk, next year I'll go to the beach, to the mountains, to the desert. Ha ha, they laugh, bouncing on the net, ha ha ha ha. A pair of cool, dry hands reaches through the net, brushes against my sweaty skin, then quickly clamps a metal band around my left thigh.

iv

Life began, they say, in the fertile valleys of the great rivers—the Ganges, the Brahmaputra, the Tigris-Euphrates, perhaps even the Mississippi, even—who knows, man has turned so much of the earth into desert—the Nile or the Rio Grande. I don't believe it. I explain it to Marsha as best I can. That the outer edges, which are firm and dry and straight and we have therefore managed to put together, are merely what we have made our way out to. They are the high bluffs above the swamps, the hills ringing the rain forest, giving us the rest and the vantage point which are what we have decided we want. But this is merely the rim of our visible universe. We look across and what do we see? The other rim. And in between?

　　"You've been working too many jig-saw puzzles," she says, though she knows that the only game I can tolerate is Scrabble, where you begin in the middle and work your way outward. She herself plays no games at all.

And in between, I repeat, pressing on, ah, in between. I lose myself in my metaphor, my eyes so bad I cannot, in fact, see across to the other side, whereas with the least motion, in the humid atmosphere of the rain forest, into which I have once more plunged, my glasses steam up, and I am forced to stop and wipe them clean before I can proceed. In between, I say, when I am ready to go on again, in between—in that dark, damp, overshadowed, soft, wet, buzzing, chirping, solemn, throbbing, undivided, bug-ridden territory—that's where it all began.

"My anthropologist! " she exclaims, in mock admiration, skipping away from the bed to open the shades and the window, letting both the afternoon sun and the cool autumn breezes into the room.

"Nothing of the sort," I respond. I disclaim any credit for scientific objectivity. It's my life I seek, down there. I wipe my glasses clean with a corner of the sheet, and hook them back over my ears. She returns to the bed, and the broad band of sunlight, only late summer in reality, not autumn yet, falls upon her body. The dark tones of her skin glow. She is continually taken for Indian or Greek, Mexican, Jewish, or, in a sari, north Indian—even, once, for black. And so passes with easy familiarity across the settled terrain while I, not knowing what it is I stand upon just now, and therefore uncertain where—or is it how—to take the next step, lag far behind, feet dragging.

No living thing, I explain, as we sit, our feet tucked beneath us, on opposite sides of the bed, its rumpled expanse between us, penetrates the earth more deeply than the roots of those rain forest giants in their search for nutrients. With what are *my* roots entangled? And when shall I leap free of it? The dances of vacationers are carefully patterned and rehearsed, from childhood on, to keep them from getting tripped up in their own feet or the feet of others. In bright plumage they rise lightly to the tops of the Eiffel Tower, the Statue of Liberty, Mt. Fiji, the Pyramid of the Sun. They dance through the halls of the Parthenon, around the observation platform of the Empire State Building, and even among the craters that pock the dry seas of the moon. And know all the words to all the songs to be sung upon their return.

Marsha, meanwhile, has lain down again. I sit, cross-legged, on the bed by her side, my own skin dull and pale beside hers. I think that I, too, would like to walk the sun-bright, solid heights—even the frozen tundra would do—if only I could find my way out of the rain forest. I think. But first the rain forest. Do I know it well enough to leave it? Am I not expected back there still? How can I know it better?

"Come *with* me," I say, leaning over her. Intended as a request, it emerges somehow as a question, flightless and unmusical. Knowing what it's like there, not only from my efforts to give shape to it, she has no questions to ask. Not without beginnings of her own has she put together the tricky, interlocking pieces that comprise the border paths she walks so surely. So carefully. She stretches in the sunlight, and I feel the vibrations her movements set up in the mattress.

"Come with *me*," she says.

V

Now I return from the rain forest. Others greet me, each other. They ask each other the same questions as always. They ask me different questions as always. I answer them as always, and then, when the questions are over, they are ready to settle down again, like the sun, which has already turned about and begun slipping away toward the south. But I have gone off by myself, into my own office, and turned on the artificial lights, and begun to plan my next journey into the rain forest. I walk about my office, watering the plants, which have done so poorly in my absence: the ferns, the rubber plant, the philodendron. This time I won't wait till summer, I'll take a midwinter vacation. It's not too early to start planning for that right now. Perhaps I won't even wait that long. Perhaps I'll quit my job. I could leave almost immediately. I am returning. Why not? It's the beginning, the real beginning. I am in a rain forest. Not a real rain forest yet, but what difference does that make? It's only a matter of weeks. Of days. I believe it will be Guatemala. Closer. Outside, already, the trees drip incessantly—actually, it is only the usual September rainy spell, and the trees are red oaks, suffering from oak wilt, a sorrowful form of dessication, the leaves dry and curl inward from the tip, turning a dirty grey-brown, there is nothing that can be done to save the trees, and where the roots of these oaks, which grow in clusters wherever they can, cross and touch and form natural grafts to feed and sustain each other, holding hands underground in the dark for mutual benefit, there also this fungus disease hurries through, from one tree to the next. As in the rain forest, everything is interwoven, below ground as well as above, knit together and green and dripping.

What is it that drips from these trees? Everything. And how heavily! From time to time a solidly buttressed giant, its branches tangled with vines and flowers, crashes suddenly to earth, tearing a hole in the green canopy above. For a moment sunlight flashes piercingly through—or, in season, a solid flood instead of the usual steady seepage—but soon enough green arms stretch out, together, from all sides, clutch at each other, seal the gap, and all is darkened and dripping again. Below, for decades, the fallen monster rots, adding its bacteria, its stench, its sagging shape (a long, low ridge gradually leveling downward, and at one end the hollow bowl where it once fitted into the earth, gradually filling up) to the forest floor. Meanwhile, I recline here, my sticky back cooling against its soggy trunk, and contemplate the red coloration of the soil, the remarkable regularity of the seasons, and the fitness of the gloom to my eyesight, or vice versa. There are parrots and orchids in the tree above me, eyes in the steamy distance, cool and objective, a spongy ground beneath carrying my vibrations outward toward the dry edges. I am in the center of the rain forest, imbedded in my flesh. An oak leaf flutters down and is quickly gathered up. Not by me.

Dreams and Propositions
or
My Life with Gravity

i DREAM

Here's how it is. There is a hole in
the night called "dream." Every night you creep up to it, very cautiously, on hands and knees, and peer in, over the edge. Far down
below you great dark clouds are rolling about, obscuring everything.
Lightning flickers among the folds of the clouds. Muffled thunder
rises from them, a sense of their thickness, the depths below them.
You can't see across to the far side of the hole. Suddenly someone
gives you a shove from behind and you go tumbling down into it. A
long fall.

From the bottom of the hole you can see, looking back up, they
aren't thunder clouds after all, there above you, but the great over-
arching underside of one single gigantic mushroom cloud, *that* cloud.
Not actually right above you, either, but spreading along the horizon,
moving in your direction, not dissolving as it grows but leaning darkly
over you, lightning darting angrily along its inner surfaces. People
scurry wildly about you, utterly speechless. You stand motionless in
the midst of their silent, darting movements lit by the silent, darting
lightning above. And then you realize that your own children are
down there with you. *Your own children!* What shelter is there for
them? Where? How to find it? Just to get through the terrible over-
shadowing forces of this one horrible black cloud is all you want, and
then you believe everything will be all right. You know of a safe place
after all, your wife is already guiding the children there, and with
relief in the knowledge that soon the ordeal will be over you turn to
join and assist them. But as you turn you see another cloud, just like
the first, rising on yet another horizon, black, lightning-lit, an entire

13

corner of the sky, or of this hole in which you are immersed, caving in on you. And you know that the far edge, that edge you couldn't see though you knew it was where shelter and safety lay, is no longer even there.

Everybody understands the value of disaster. The sky falls but *you* learn. At least you learn that the sky can fall. No, you learn that the sky *is* falling. You learn that the sky is always falling and that you reside at the bottom of its fall. You learn to duck your head, you learn to run a zig-zag pattern among the falling chunks, to minimize harm, to judge the force of the winds, to watch for signs. Looking up, you learn to observe the passages of light and dark, the design and movement of clouds, the flight of birds. You learn to understand that you will never learn the art of prediction.

Nothing is sensible. Religion, philosophy, science, and Ralph Waldo Emerson notwithstanding, the indiscriminate actions of death, disease, and natural catastrophe continue as always. Dirt wages unceasing war on all mankind. No sooner is the furniture dusted, the floor mopped, the carpet vacuumed, the clothes cleaned, the dishes washed, than the persistence of dirt makes it necessary to do all these things all over again. Over and over and over. The diefenbachia I tended with loving care has lost all its leaves, while the coleus, ignored, rages away in a far corner of the house like a floral epidemic. Snow falls in the neighbor's yard and mine alike. The woman who loved me while I went merrily on my way, paying no attention to her, now despises me, now that I have fallen madly, wildly, in love with her. The sun itself, as we are constantly reminded, is merely a dying star. Unless something is done about all this chaos, I shall probably put a bullet through my head. Even that is senseless: merely an attempt, as unconvincing as it would probably be unsuccessful, to indicate how I consider interjecting my own bit of chaos into the world's.

iv   DREAM

I awake on the far edge, my usual self, trying to write down these things, certain propositions that will give order to my dreams and relief to the great weight with which they burden me, only to discover that the far edge appears to have been vastly overrated. There is very little there. Here. Such propositions as I manage to devise intrude here not with order but with a chaos of their own, leaning down over me (random lightning flickering along their undersides) with such density that I feel their great weight even before the actual moment of contact. Does the far edge, I wonder, also have a far edge? If that is where I am headed, since I seem to be in motion, in slow and heavy motion, what will I find there, and who? Where are my children? In another world, obviously. I pause to quote myself: "another world." That doesn't sound right. It is, I believe, technically correct, but not "right." I do not feel right, nor am I able to judge the rightness of what I am experiencing. My body and my mind process the material of my experience alike, and all that passes through me emerges, in slow time, in the form of these small, dense, and perfectly formed little words. Meanwhile, I continue to move along in the darkness, arrive at the edge of yet another hole, perhaps the same hole, lean over, waiting for the inevitable surprise of the inevitable shove from behind. The long fall. Yes, the same hole of course. One goes through it over and over again, as best one can. It is still night. The nights on this planet are so unbelievably long that if one waited for the dawn in order to continue his journey, one would be an old man before the light broke. It isn't worth discussing. You go when you can and when you can't, you stop. Day or night. The days, for their part, are as long as the nights, far longer than anyone can continue making progress through. No one can stand so much light. A day and a night together are an eternity. The hardest part is remembering that yesterday was just such another eternity, that tomorrow. . . .

v   PROPOSITION

Nothing happens in the past. How, therefore, shall I tell my tale of grief and woe? Retail it rather, since I got it wholesale from Edgar Allan Poe. Is it my fault the same things happen to us all? Poe! I was there first, it was the past after all, in the dark all pasts look alike and the past, as you discovered, is the worst thing that can happen—keep happening—to us, time sweeps its dust indiscriminately over us all, dirties the residence, clogs the pores, makes breathing difficult, you just happen to have written about it before I did.

This is the past, then, and nothing happens here. You can dream it afresh every night and nothing will be changed, nothing. It is, on the contrary, a frozen world, where everything *has* happened, a dead world, like another planet, a world without possibilities in which the time traveler risks permanent entrapment, a world where there is no freedom to be because whatever might have been has been foreclosed by what *has* been. A world where the truly living are walled up by the living dead. "For the love of God, Montresor!" But Montresor cannot hear me. He is a denizen of the past, for whom everything has already happened; he just goes on doing the same thing, the thing that constitutes *his* past, over and over again. It's all he knows or is. But look at what he's doing to my present, my future!Must we always be in the hands of the past like this? I'm deathly afraid, and not without good reason. Soon the last brick will be mortared into place, and all will go dark. What a fool I am to subscribe to such notions. It's all in the mind, isn't it, merely in the mind. Of course. But what's that I keep hearing? The past scrapes away at its work, ugly sounds. I shake my head. Tiny bells jingle in the darkness.

vi   PROPOSITION

If you don't make up your own mind, then someone else will.
If you don't control your own mind, then someone else will.
If you don't exploit your own mind, then someone else will.
If you don't explore your own mind, then someone else will.
If you don't deplore your own mind, then someone else will.
If you don't abandon your own mind, then some else will.
Begin here.

vii   DREAM

Actually, my dreams are mostly about people, ordinary people. They wax their cars in the shade by the side of the road, bring flowers home to brighten the house, fill the washing machine with dirty clothes and dial the proper settings. I look on, amazed. In the real world I pull the station wagon out beneath the shade of the elms, rub the heavy wax onto its finish, wait fifteen minutes according to the instructions, then, with a clean, dry cloth, begin slowly to wipe the dried paste off. Two neighbors emerge simultaneously from their separate houses, a variety of children collecting about them as they meet on the sidewalk and advance upon me. One admires, with surprise, the rich, gleaming blue revealed as I polish off the dry wax; the other, a man somewhat older than myself, remembers fondly how his father used to do the same thing on Saturday afternoons, but cannot recall ever having done it himself. My wife is pleased with the roses I have brought home but also amused, since I have never done such a thing before. Moreover, what will we put them in? And where is the best place in the house for them? The children want to know, "Why do we have flowers today?" "Isn't that strange?" My would-be stockbroker wants to know why I want to invest in today's market. It's his opinion I would be much better off keeping my money in the savings and loan. All my underwear emerges from the wash slightly blue; I have gotten someone's new cotton sock mixed in with the whites. In my dreams I stand cautiously aside, a mere observer, watching ordinary people do the ordinary things, and I am, as I realize when they pause in their activities to glance up at me, slightly ridiculous. And doing the ordinary things, I am, as I quickly realize when other people pause to observe me, also slightly ridiculous.

viii   DREAM

When I finally realized that the most significant events were those that happened to the most people with the greatest frequency, I came to understand that the dramatic form best suited to the fullest expression of the human condition could be nothing other than the soap opera. Here, I saw, as nowhere else, was where fathers encountered sons, mothers daughters, hosts guests, doctors patients, students teachers, businessmen secretaries, husbands wives, wives lovers, lovers husbands, lawyers clients, over and over again. And why not? It was true. It was ordinary. It was what happened.

It was just like life. It was, moreover, the single most enduring form to have appeared, and remained, on the public communications media of my time. In it events occurred with such a graceful and predictable slow motion—each individual revelation, confession, or confrontation stretching out for days, or even weeks—that it became easily possible to step in between the discrete moments that made up each event. Once there, I could get the feel of them from all sides, and ultimately come to know the smooth surface of each— before the next stage of the unfolding event edged carefully into the foreground—with a sense of fullness that I could never gain about similar moments in my own existence, which hurried by far too rapidly for it to be possible to hae such a satisfying experience of them. Time was what it was possible to find all one needed of there. Time for the fine, long moments of anguish, time for the slow radiation of an item of of information outward in all directions, time for the vast gap opening up between a moment of departure and one of arrival. This was what was, this was what one could relish getting into. Where acts of violence were rare, worries common. That was the way things really were.

ix PROPOSITION

Accidents happen. They intrude themselves like ugly and self-demonstrative propositions. People fall, just like the sky—observed, ignored, with cries or in silence, alone or together or both. Airplanes fall from the sky, window cleaners from skyscrapers, children from swings, great soccer crowds through collapsing bleachers, mountaineers, construction workers, the rich, the well-born, the famous, the safe. Mine shafts collapse. Knives slip. Oil heaters blow up. Rusty hot water pipes burst. Forgotten images, or ones you thought safely defused, explode suddenly, in your mind, in the middle of the night.

x   PROPOSITION

Everybody is somebody special.

"Why?" cries my lover's best friend, banging down her cup so that the coffee, dark as my lover's hair, sloshes onto the white table cloth, staining it with round spots dark as my lover's nipples.

"Why?" she cries again, her voice and eyes so dark with alarm that the waitress comes hurrying toward us, veering away only at the last moment, when I hold up my hand in the signal to Stop, toward the one other table still occupied at this odd midafternoon hour.

Then she levels the charge of her voice and eyes at me: "You're nobody special! "

Should I feel wounded by such a charge? I'm not young or tall or handsome or witty. Not rich or clever or famous. For what, then, her eyes demand, is that able and beautiful woman my lover risking her marriage, her family, career, home, future, happiness . . . ? The waitress hovers two tables away, reading, I think, my mind. And this friend, this woman able and beautiful herself, gazes at me with a sort of passion of her own, wanting, I think, less an answer to her "Why?" than some mystic assurance that I am, after all, somebody special, that I am not just another wanderer in the dark, another slow learner and ignorant dreamer, another curious time traveler messing around in the slow dimensions of reality—that her friend's insane risk is worth it after all, though she, who has known me years longer than her friend, our mutual friend, should surely know better than to seek assurances of *that* sort.

xi   DREAM

"There are certain themes of which the interest is all absorbing, but which are too entirely horrible for the purposes of legitimate fiction. . . . To be buried alive is, beyond question, the most terrific of those extremes which has ever fallen to the lot of mere mortality."—E.A. Poe

All problems are formal problems. The mathematics of disaster, which in most cases can be reduced to two solid bodies moving together at predictable speeds, can generally be given as a simple formula. Nothing could be more predictable than my rate of fall from the edge to the bottom of the hole, unless it could be the effect of the final impact, the explosion of words, dreams, propositions, their rate of fallout and pattern of dispersion. The calculation of the volume of oxygen contained in a given area sealed off from the outside, and the precise limits of life it could sustain. Opportunities for survival on an alien planet. Arrangements and rearrangements of a given number of figures in a given amount of space over a given period of time, as well as the possible effects of the introduction of yet another figure . . . and another . . . and another. . . . The encounter with the unknown. The sudden recognition of the obvious. Nothing happens in the past. Recognition is a hole in the night and one creeps ever so cautiously to the edge, considering depths, rates of fall, distances around or across, whole populations below, on whom it may well seem the sky is falling. Like Alice, one continues to consider the formal aspects of the problem even as one falls: "Do cats eat rats . . . ?" Where in the entire house is the most advantageous spot to display these flowers? Exactly how many bricks does it take to wall up an undefined possibility, how many hard, sharp-edged words to tunnel a fresh exit? What obvious chain of thought expands these dark, round coffee stains on the tablecloth into you? The children, ah, the children. All problems are formal problems, but they are all filled with people who have dreams whose central proposition is the chaos that fractures the formal order they are living.

The important thing to remember about all these people is their fragility.

A fire burns in the yard, alongside the house, slowly consuming a strip of lawn about six feet wide which runs from the street in front of the house to the line of red oaks which mark the rear boundary of the lot. Although there are no flames to be seen, a dense black cloud of smoke rises along this line, hovering darkly over our house and the neighbor's alike. Using an old garden spade I attempt to dig into this strip of smouldering ground in order to reach, and extinguish, the source of the conflagration, but the further I dig the more I realize that this is not just a surface fire, burning along a wide swatch of dry grass, but an intense underground blaze, the kind one reads about that burns incessantly beneath the peat bogs, deep and slow and unquenchable. Below the dry and ashy ground that crumbles away at the touch of my spade, I see its red, flameless glow, extending not just along the visibly charred surface strip but beneath the very spot I am standing on, green as it still is, and beneath the house itself, and perhaps beneath the entire neighborhood, smouldering steadily away, as perhaps it has been for years, while the dark cloud that is merely its current manifestation hangs heavily over everything, so dense it seems that chunks could break loose from it and crumble, like ashes, into the yard below, and when I look away from its oppressive weight I see you leaning out of the second-floor window. You clearly want to offer help, to say something helpful, to ask if there is anything you can do. But this is not your dream, and so there is nothing you can say.

XV　DREAM

That man over there in the corner, behind the sofa, the one gathering twigs and bits of string, bent straws and crumpled paper napkins, pulling loose threads from men's pants cuffs and the hems of women's skirts . . . that's the one I mean, the one you saw outside yesterday waxing his car in the hot sunshine, quite contrary to the instructions on the can, while dark thunderclouds piled up on the western horizon; the one who is walled up in here tonight, among these masked revelers, most of whom he actually knows, while life rages continually away outside; the one who crawls around on all fours here among the legs of these party-goers slouching together on sofas, sliding from the arms of chairs into each other's laps, leaning against walls, pianos, and door jambs with their hands full of drinks and sandwiches; who is gathering, as he progresses slowly about the room, scraps of torn paper, fluffy bits of dog hair, discarded cigarettes, kleenex, bread crusts; whose wife is in the basement, dancing, and whose lover sits in the kitchen sipping coffee with her decorous and well-costumed husband; who worries, as he crawls along through here, about his children and thinks frequently in terms of propositions: *things fall.* What he is doing, which makes him so easily recognizable here in the act of picking things up, is exercising his dream of being comfortable wherever he is. He has titled this dream "Landscape with Nesting Figure."

xvi   PROPOSITION

One certainly has to dream a lot of dreams to get through a lifetime. And having dreamed them, one is not yet finished, either; they still have to be lived. Nor is living them the end, for that matter. One crawls about among them armed with chaos, like a toy gun, and waiting to see what happens.

xvii   DREAM

We are about to commit an intuitive act. I know the feeling, the enormous pressure, that immediately precedes it, dense and static as a proposition, building up heavily inside me, ready to burst forth, to become reality. What was that "troubled dream" that Gregor Samsa was dreaming just before he woke up to find himself changed into an enormous insect? He was dreaming, of course, that he had woken up and found himself changed into an enormous insect. Think of the pressures of such a monstrous dream! What else could he do but confirm it with his life? He woke up: "This was no dream." We burst forth into daily life full of the enormity burgeoning inside us. We are about to commit an intuitive act, not something thought out but something from within, emerging whether we will it or not on the strength of powers not the powers of our minds. And yet the nature of our vision—do we see this emergent act? is there anything to be done about it? do we *want* to try to do anything about it—perhaps confuses us, ever so slightly. For a moment we see ourselves poised, an exhibit from the Museum of Natural History. Early Man. The male is leaning toward a ragged fire, the shank bone of some deerlike animal in his hand. The female sits close by, holding in her outstretched hand the sharp stone with which she is about to scrape the inside of the hide spread out before her. A scene of ponderous deliberation. On the rocky ledge above and behind them crouches an enormous sabre-toothed tiger. We wake up suddenly and with a feeling of great relief. I am standing at the stove, about to use the spatula in my hand to turn the two hamburgers sizzling in the frying pan. You are carefully separating and folding the clothes you have just brought up from the laundry. The room is filled with the brightness of clean laundry, the smell of frying hamburger, the feeling that something of great magnitude is about to happen. That, perhaps, the toy tiger we bought in India many years ago is about to spring on us from its perch atop the refrigerator. It suddenly becomes very difficult to catch our breath. We dream the past and wake to find ourselves buried alive inside that airless dream. And then we have the nerve to ask how we happen to be there.

xviii PROPOSITION

No system can explain itself (says Goedel's Theorem), but we keep on trying, believing it's the least we can dream of doing for ourselves: so that when we wake up, on the far side of wherever we were, we know that the system that wakes us *is* ourselves. We have been there before. It's in the mind. And then, perhaps, since nothing is sensible, since we have met both the dream as a self-sustaining proposition and the special, fragile, and ordinary people who wander around in it, since we have all gasped for breath together in its slow and airless time and begun to learn some of the right moves for staying alive under its falling skies, we don't have to sit around waiting for explanations after all. We only have to know what happens.

The Land of Milk
and Honey

The River Jordan's deep and wide, and it must take quite a boat to get to the other side, and I used to think, once upon a time, that I had found just the thing. Oh crossings! It was Christmas eve and I had just gotten out of the hospital and there was a big move coming up, to a distant city, and who knew what that would bring or even, with all that was piling up around us, how it would be done. Who knew? Oh we had made such crossings of great magnitude before—and usually, like this one, in response to some urge of mine—but somehow, perhaps because of the season or the sickness or the sheer size of the crossing ahead, this particular conglomeration of events came to seem to me, as I moved uncomfortably about in their midst, the painful pull of my stitches tugging at my guts, like a condensation of my life, for at their center was that perennial question for all crossings: How are you going to make it?

When I though of answers that others had come up with, the only one that kept coming to mind was old Satchel Paige's, that he just kept looking back over his shoulder. Well, I tried looking back—who was I to neglect any possibilities that might help me to get on over?—but what did I see? Perhaps there should have been some ogres on my tail, just to make things easier, but the fact was that every time I looked around there simply wasn't anything to be seen. Neither my father nor the ghost of my mother nor my fellow employees, young or old, nor my wife and children were back there yapping at my heels as I strolled to the river bank. If I had just looked about me, instead of only behind, no doubt I would have seen that they were on both sides of me—equally curious as to how I was going to make it. I was ready to go, but, even after all those past crossings, from one place, one time, to another, what did I know? It occurs to me just now, thinking of myself standing there, that as a scrawny and generally nonparticipatory high school student the one athletic prowess I had managed to cultivate to the level of varsity excellence was swimming. Slim and speedy I was, at my best in the short sprints, and the pools, of course, were only twenty-five yards long. But that particular talent had long since fallen into disuse, it was time to move ahead, and the river before me, as I say, was deep and wide.

I was undergoing a painful and dismayingly lengthy recuperation from what was, after all, only minor surgery. A variety of friends had brought me, well in advance, glowing tales of immediate recoveries, by themselves or others of their acquaintance, from similar hernia operations; the doctor insisted that I would be engaging in all normal activities within a few days after the operation; and aside from this slight breach in the abdominal wall I was, all agreed, a reasonably healthy specimen of an adult male. All right then, I had said, I'll go and get it over with. But the problem was that it was not over with. I had endured, in the name of a speedy recovery, the first painful steps down the hospital corridor less than twenty-four hours after the operation, violent spasms of intestinal gas, the groggy inability to read even one of the books I had brought up to the hospital with me—I'll do that too, I had said when I left for the hospital, of those previously impenetrable volumes—as well as inedible food, insufficient sedatives, painful messages from my children, who seemed to be under the impression that I had gone off somewhere to die, and the humiliation, and relief, when I was at last discharged, of being carted off to the waiting car in a wheelchair. At home, unable to climb the stairs, I was bedded down on the living room day bed, from which I frequently groaned and stumbled my way to the bathroom and at last, three days later, to our second floor bedroom.

By then it was Christmas eve, and though each time I moved a frightful pain leapt up out of my groin to scream at me that I was not Santa Claus, there were still certain things to be done before dawn. What a mountain of wrapping!I don't know how you ever managed it. But also there was Nick's gas station to be assembled from scratch. And Annie's dollhouse. I'll do it, I said, going through the least painful gyrations I could manage to prop my back against the headboard and spread out before and around me the thin sheets of instructions and the dozens of intricately interlocking metal pieces. On the bed-side table was a glass of scotch, but that was more painful to reach out for than were those hunks of brightly enameled metal, each of them poorly shaped for its function, improperly stamped out, inadequately accounted for in the instructions, and bearing—like ogres not of the past but of the future: do it then, like you said you would, if you dare—sharp, evil little edges, capable of, successful at, ripping my numb and fumbling fingers to shreds.

And beyond that, beyond the gas station and the dollhouse, beyond, for that matter, the operation and Christmas, but hauling them outward in its wake, like the lead beast in a pack of wild dogs, the kind I remember them putting poisoned meat out for in the streets of Mexican villages while begging the owners of tame pets to keep them well locked up for the day, roamed the threat of that impending move, the stacks of still-empty or partly filled cartons that were its major manifestations dumped randomly about the bedroom, leaning against the walls on the staircase landing and in the hallways, spilling into every conceivable corner of the house, under tables, on top of cabinets, even in the bathtub. There were, for us, no tame beasts at that time, nothing we could keep locked up, or, to get back to that preferred metaphor, no rivers that weren't in flood; this whole present-cum-future surged along under our—all right, then, my—feet like a flagrant but mostly petty challenge—no crusades to be carried out here, no victories to be won, no glories gained, just a job—and Satch was no help and neither was Heraclitus—who wanted to step into *that* twice?—and I just kept on stupidly saying, I'll do it, I'll do it.

Amazingly enough, I did.

That, then, was when I thought I had found just the thing for getting across. For in spite of one thing and another, Christmas came on Christmas morning, and both the gas station and the dollhouse lay brightly gleaming beneath the tree with only, perhaps, a slight smear of blood here and there that I had failed to wipe off, giving any indication of the struggle. And eventually I was back on my feet and moving as painlessly, if slightly more potbellied, as before. And we were at last safely settled in St. Paul, housed, schooled, befriended, and a few random tributaries spanned along the way. And if the Mississippi—to say nothing of the Jordan—still lay before, us, and uncrossed as yet, at this strange northern latitude, though there had been occasions in the past when we had passed over it with blithe indifference, further south, why, that was simply because you didn't have to cross the Mississippi to get to St. Paul from that land of post-operative depression and midholiday dismay and pretravel chaos and packing cartons and car repair and trailer rental and house cleaning where I had discovered that all you have to do, if you really want to do something, is to *do it.*

ii

The Mississippi. The Mississippi in history. Mark Twain on the Mississippi as an arterial highway. The Mississippi in sixth-grade social studies books. The headwaters of the Mississippi; sixth graders in Minnesota learn that as well: Lake Itasca, at whose gently flowing northern outlet may be found a series of stepping stones whereon even the smallest child can skip easily across that fearful demon of the floodplains, the Father of Waters. I, for one, have never been there. Already, as far north as St. Paul, the river is no longer the broad and mysterious expanse that most Americans conceive it to be, the great brown god of its poets. Hemmed in by bluffs and choked up by locks and dams and falls and islands, with its two sides securely stitched together by going on two dozen bridges between the southeast edge of St. Paul and the northwest corner of Minneapolis, it is neither so wide as this nor so deep as that, and though it will do, come springtime, to spill a bit of water on the low-lying areas—closing off a few roads, muddying up a few warehouses, temporarily un-housing a few stubborn riverside residents, who will be back shortly—still it is on the whole, a slow, pleasant, easy-going . . . stream.

That I came to take such notice of it was wholly the doing of friends, for surely I lived at that time in an ignorance of rivers and had, indeed, just come from a town that wholly lacked one. A city without a river? I have just looked it up in the atlas, fearing for a moment that maybe I had only been blind to it all that time, but no, it's true. This new one had its river, though, for Roger came and took us—or rather led us, for there were too many of us to fit in one car, and he absconded with a child or two in his while the rest of us followed along—there on Sunday mornings. We stuck to the east bank, parking at last somewhere along the winding boulevard that follows the bluffs there, and then regrouped to walk along the boulevard itself, above the river, or to take one of the many accesses—a dirt road leading to a boat landing area, stairways and cemented walks contributed and cared for by the WPA and the Parks Department, respectively, or, less frequently, steep twisting dirt paths which, to judge by the number of people we always found along them—children, lovers, bird watchers, boy scouts, the middle aged and elderly—received the most use of all—down to the edge of the river itself.

From the boulevard the river was a quiet, distant, dimly brown . . . presence would be too much to say for it, since there continually fluttered around me, between me and it, the conversation of the adults—Marsha, Roger, perhaps George, who stuck to the east bank because he feared bridges, and Sandy, who was happy to walk anywhere—and the playfulness of the children, heaving piles of leaves into the air on our fall walks or, in the winter, hiding behind trees to pelt us with snowballs. And the dog, that great unruly beast of a St. Bernard whom we were somehow always obliged to bring along—there was a presence for you!—whose function seemed to be to tug me, at the other end of the leash, this way and that, according to his whims or his needs, so that not for long at any one time was I ever able to focus on the children, or the adults, or, especially, the river. And at the river's edge, when we walked down there, it was no better, for the distractions above were compounded by the hazards below: the children scrambling out on half-fallen trees that hung out over the river, adults slipping and sliding and talking their way along the pebbly bank, the struggle to maneuver among the litter of beer cans and broken glass and, at the same time, to keep the dog from plunging into the water, and hauling me along after him. With such preoccupations was the nearness of the Mississippi effectively fogged over, so that though I was aware of the steady, solid motion of that dark body of water beside me, and only slightly below eye level, it might as well have been, for all the conscious grasp I had of it—was I not, after all, busy enough hanging onto my friends, my family, my dog?—on another planet, a thin blue line in some yet unopened *Geography of Venus*. And its other side . . . was there, indeed, another side to it? Every once in a while my eyes were lifted, by the children's cries or gestures, to see, over there, a picnic fire on a sandy beach or a cave in the side of the bluffs, but that was a function of the children, not of the river.

The more I walked there, then, in Sunday ritual, the less I actually came to know of the river. For all of George's lectures on the frailty of the underpinnings of the Lake Street bridge and its immanent collapse, Roger's knowledgeable running commentary on agate pebbles and sandstone caves and high water marks, the children's reckless hanging out over it on rotten branches or the dog's equally reckless attempts to drink of it, what lay out there beside us—me— was less a river than merely an indifferent adjunct to these walks, like a street, or someone's front lawn.

What I needed, I decided one summer midweek morning in a solemn moment of contemplation, when various vacations and activities had kept us from the river for several Sundays in a row and I was brought around at last in my thinking from an awareness of the absence of companionship to an awareness of the absence of . . . something else, was a drama of events that would give the presence of the river a reality that, so far, I had found more of in the planning of our walks than in the actual taking of them. So with you at work and the children out at play, I ignored the uncut grass and the unweeded garden and the many other tasks that I had laid out for the week—though I would do them all, to be sure, for I knew how to *do* things—and began to construct for myself a possible future with a real river in it.

It went like this: We would be walking along the bank, in our usual crowd, when sudden cries would reach us from out on the water, where a canoe had overturned, leaving one occupant still clinging to it while the other was swept away, downstream; quickly kicking off my shoes and tossing aside my shirt—I could never quite decide what to with my glasses—I would plunge in, stroke rapidly across to the helpless one, tow him or her to the opposite, now nearer, shore, then return for the canoe and the one still clinging to it. Or, it would be wintertime, and from where we walked along the bluffs I would see a group of children venturing out on the frozen surface of the river, and would go plunging down the steep bank after them even before the first one had broken through the thin ice at mid-stream. Or, at long last the Lake Street bridge, just upstream from where we were walking that day, would begin to crumble, swaying in slow motion as the ancient timbers that supported the eastern edge began to buckle and splinter, and as the first car slipped over its side and plunged toward the water, I would already be marking the spot where it would go under, throwing off my clothes. . . . The possibilities were almost limitless. The one thing that they all had in common was the notion that I could meet that river, or, for that matter, any river, on the terms of its own reality, and even cross it, if need be, when I came to it. And why not?

In fact, it happened like this. On that same hot Thursday after-noon, without a thought for the children or the hour, I rushed the dog into the car and set out alone for a river that had never existed before. I could easily have met it at one of the usual places, finding it anew with no trouble at all, but I chose instead to meet it in a place where we had never walked before but which Roger had sometimes spo-ken of: on an island that rested in the confluence of the Mississippi and the Minnesota rivers and was reached by first crossing the Mis-sissippi, on one of those cumbersome concrete bridges from whose center lanes the river can't even be seen, then taking a winding side road that ducks down underneath the highway and slips into the little state park at the foot of the bluffs, and finally crossing on foot over a small earth-filled causeway onto the island itself.

Perhaps because it was midweek, and so hot, the park was deserted, though it was cooled by a multitude of shade trees and, at that hour of the afternoon, by the shadow of the bluffs. Along one side of the park, beyond the picnic tables, flowed the Mississippi. I had crossed it, but, as I now crossed over to it, it still lay before me, quiet as ever. Even the dog was quiet. He settled massively down beside me as I lay down on the bank, letting his leash hang loosely from my wrist. For the first time, sitting there, bent slightly forward, I found myself truly at eye level with the river, and was struck by the peculiar vision that it humped up slightly at midstream. And there was the opposite bank. I could see children scrambling down its steep slope, hanging onto bushes as they slipped and slid, their cries coming sharply across the water to me, a dog romping with them, barking, and a man and a woman standing by the edge of the water below them. It could have been me, you, us. And what a weight there was to the motion of that dark water between. It was a gentle stream, yes. It moved ever so slowly, yes. But *how* it moved! Could it possibly do for me to venture out onto, or into, that? I had crossed it, yes. Now that I thought about it, I recalled that of course I had crossed it, many times already, between the two cities. But here I was, for the first time, at the level of its own reality. And to make a crossing there, well, that would really be doing something!

But what was I going to do: strip and take two hundred pounds of dog and my own potbelly out into that soft swirl of brown water and trust us all, yes and you too, to my long-unpracticed crawl stroke? The other shore might still have been the far bank of a river on Venus, for as much as I was likely to do that. Here I was across the river and the other shore still as distant as before, as unreal; the people I had momentarily stopped watching were gone now and there was not a sound to be heard from over there. And in between? What was there about this river that I hadn't reckoned with, that made me feel as I did, that finally even made me stand up, brushing off the seat of my pants and taking a firmer hold on the dog's leash, and look around behind me, for those ogres who might have conveniently shown up then to drive me out into the river, with sticks and fire? But the park was empty. If there was any danger, it certainly wasn't back there, behind me. And if what I really wanted was to be over there, on the other side of the river, then all I had to do was to do it: climb in my car and drive back up to the highway and over the bridge and down the river road, leave the car again and climb down the slope to the water. Nothing could be easier. There I would be, in a very short time, looking across that sluggish muddy flow to the other side, where there was a small park and, perhaps, a man in it, with a dog. . . . What I did instead, was to turn and walk through the park, that oversized beast trotting beside me, tongue hanging from the side of his mouth, and cross the causeway onto the island which, out of the shadow of the bluffs, was still bathed in sunlight. And wide, overgrown with tall grasses, bordered with trees, and unbelievably hot. Wanting to get across it, and down to one of the rivers again, or preferably both, at the point where they came together, I did not linger long at the edge, for there was a rotten, unpleasant stench that hung in the hot air there and the trees, though both tall and broad, showed only a meager amount of green. If they had carried sufficient foliage to provide some shade, I might have stayed beneath them, and gone around the perimeter of the island, but they were dry and for the most part appeared lifeless, carrying tangled high in their branches, far above my head, not a crown of green leaves but ragged clumps of grey and rotting matter left there by the high waters of last spring's flood, and so I turned away to cut across the center of the island. With the dog pacing along behind me at the end of his chain, I plunged into the dry grasses beyond the trees, in the direction I thought most likely to take me quickly across the island, but the island was large and the grasses high; they bent easily before me but leapt up quickly after my passage, caught and cracked in my shoes and sweat-drenched clothing, tangled in the dog's coat, offered no vantage point from which I could see over them, and only after a long long time showed any sign of thinning out. What they opened on, however, was not either of the shorelines, but a gigantic mound of rocks, no, small pebbles, where I was glad enough to let myself down, for though it was even hotter here than among the grasses, it was, at least, a clearing. I would have happily let the dog off the leash, to find his own comfort, had it not been for the fear that he would have disappeared at once into the surrounding grasses, on his own quest for the river. Instead, I fingered his leash idly in one hand and, with the other, began to examine the pebbles on which I sat. Beneath a thin coating of dust, they were nicely polished, often brightly colored, even a few small agates among them, but so many of them, so many! And in that beautiful, almost symmetrical mound.

And at that hour! Suddenly, seeing the pace at which the sun was dropping down toward the bluffs that were again visible from where I sat on the side of the mound, I realized how late it was. And, in a manner of speaking, where I was: right in the middle of the river. For what did all that smelly debris high up in those trees back there mean except that, floodtime, this whole flat island was entirely covered by water? and this mound, then, a handful of whose pebbles I held in my hand, was no doubt where the two rivers met, in flood, and swirled about, together, depositing as they did so something of the load each carried desperately along at that season. One of the rocks I examined in that handful was a graceful, softly polished curve, about an inch and a half long and a half inch in thickness, banded, along its length, with the muted colors of the rainbow. This one I kept, standing up, pocketing it, letting the others drop back onto the mound, giving a tug at the leash and waiting for the dog to scramble clumsily back to his feet.

And this time *he* took the lead as we headed back in the direction of the bluffs, tugging me along, in his usual fashion, at a much greater pace than I liked. But he flattened a path through the grass and seemed to have a reasonably good idea of where he was headed, which was more than I had managed to give much evidence of before, so it was no surprise when we suddenly burst out of the high grass onto the tops of some large rocks at the foot of which was a narrow stretch of sand fronting the river, the Mississippi again, for there just a short way upstream was the edge of the park where I had sat, and, reaching from bluff to bluff farther on, the concrete bridge, and suddenly, here, that huge dog gave a single tremendous lunge forward, pulled me tumbling down the cracked face of the rocks, jerked the leash free from my hand, and, while I sat back up on the beach at the foot of the rocks, groaning and rubbing my bruised hands and knees and trying to see how the torn shreds of my pants legs could be fitted back together, went plunging on into the river, where I saw him, when I had at last got my glasses adjusted back on my face, standing chest deep in that muddy water and drinking and drinking and drinking.

iii

That was all there was to it. I had created a future for myself in which there was the real presence of a river, but when I had come up to it, face to face, it was difficult to know just what, if anything, to do with it. The truth was, I neither struck out boldly across it on my own nor had the excuse of being driven into it from behind. Quite to the contrary, the children were disappointed at my having gone off to the river and left them behind, and the rainbow-colored stone with whose beauty I attempted to mollify them only served to whet their appetites and sharpen their pain; you were angry, not at my being late for dinner or even at my leaving the children behind, but at my having gone off for hours—could it have really been so long?—and left no word behind; my clothes were ruined, my bruises were turning painfully toward the violet end of the spectrum, and the dog was soon to come down with a severe intestinal malady that cost us a good bit of money, and almost cost him his life. And all this, also, was as much a part of the future I had created as I had supposed that river might be, and it was not at all clear what I was to do with it. So I had made a place in my world for a real river from what I had taken before to be a wholly alien landscape, and I had closed in upon it, after a fashion. That much I did, I suppose, but what could I do them? What had I really done, with my decision to *do*? Was it worth it and where was I, and where were all the others, when it was over? What

sort of stupidity had I committed in pushing as I did for even so insignificant a future as this that I did not think you were a part of? That
was no crossing, was it? Or was it? If I learned anything, it was that, in
the end, it would all have to be done over again. It wouldn't be the
same, of course, but it would be back to the river, for sure. Not to do
anything with it, perhaps, but to take what chances there were to
take with it. Sooner or later. For us.

   Meanwhile, it is perhaps more than an idle curiosity to recount
how, alone or with you or with others, I have crossed lots of other
rivers, both before and after this time. Like the Ohio, twice a day,
five days a week, and sometimes more, for some six years running,
between Cincinnati and Covington, plus random passes before and
after, most of them, until the recent construction of the new interstate
highway bridge, on the wooden-floored suspension bridge completed in 1865 under the watchful, experimental eye of John August
Roebling, as a prelude to his more memorable crossing into Brook-
lyn. And the East River myself, and the Hudson, too, over and under
both. And the St. Lawrence at Quebec, where what was at issue was
not the river but the ancient bus, and would it hold together long
enough to get us across. And the Mississippi at New Orleans, at Mem-
phis, and at St. Louis, working north. And the Columbia, going
south, in such a muddle of children and driving that it was not until
miles beyond that I realized we must have already made, back there
somewhere, the crossing I had been looking forward to all morning.
And the Seine and the Tiber, on many bridges each, though I came
at last to conclude that as rivers they weren't much; they just happened to be well located. And more exotic yet, the Ganges, in a flat-
bottomed scow that, now that I think about it, never did take us
across but only up and down, along the ghats, where the steps came
down to the edge of that thickly laden water whose liquid poison is
bottled and sold as a charm against all the world's evils and where,
indeed, on that sluggish, heavy, earth-colored, and yet mobile mass,
it seemed that one might be able to keep on walking, right across its
surface. And a small tributary of the Pampanadi in, believe it or not,
a hollowed-out log. And the wide Chao Phraya, in violently choppy

water and an antique, overcrowded tourist boat that began leaking
so badly on the return crossing that, with great pools of brown water
sloshing back and forth between the children's feet as we lurched
clumsily toward the still-distant dock, a veritable flood of anxiety
washed the Dawn Temple itself, the very goal of that reckless pilgrim-
age—O tourists! tourists!—right out of my mind. And the Mekong,
but at such an altitude that only by looking at a chart of our route did
I make the discovery, in the past tense once again, that we had already crossed it. And then the Mississippi again, north, at St. Paul.
The order is one of ascending danger. And ascending possibility.

But we never have crossed the Jordan, though once upon a
time, when we left the whole Mississippi Valley behind for a year of
travel, we surely came close enough. We had left Tel Aviv for Bom-
bay at twilight on a lovely summer evening, and though the plane
was several hours behind schedule, nonetheless a direct route should
have taken us over the Jordan in less than an hour after takeoff and
at something like twenty thousand feet. Quite a crossing, indeed! But
the political situation decreed otherwise, and planes departing from
Israel were not permitted to cross Jordanian—or Egyptian, or Le-
banese—borders, which meant that there was no direct route from
here to there, even for American citizens in an American jetliner, as
perhaps we should have known, and that we could not cross the
Jordan after all—or, for that matter, the Nile, the Tigris, or the Eu-
phrates—and that when we should have been sailing grandly east-
ward across the Jordan in a great silver ship, we were, instead,
backtracking westward out over the Mediterranean and banking
north over Cyprus and only then, at last, in such a roundabout fashion, turning east, across Turkey, and into the night. Hallelujah. And
it is in the midst of the graceful curvature of that flight—the very first,
lest I forget to note it, on that route for that airline—with the three
children shoeless and blanketed and stretched out asleep each across
his own row of seats in the darkened, almost empty (why? is there
something about an inaugural flight that makes people hesitant to
take it?) cabin, and you wrapped up sleeping in a smaller place, but
closer to me, and only the crew awake but already, no doubt, hum-

ming along in the quiet routine of long-distance flights, and the hours of the night ripping away beneath our eastbound rush at a vastly accelerated pace, that I often see myself still: a myopic beast wide awake in the very depths of the night and watchful—watchful of the darkness outside the window, and of each of you bundled up in sleep around me, and of the instrumentation behind the closed bulkhead up in front and the delays out of which we had risen and the dotted line of our passage as it showed on the airline map, crossing riverless deserts and seas, and of the dawn soon to blossom for us over that vast continent ahead—and ready for nothing. And everything.

The Beast in the Jungle vs.
A Sense of the Comic

The edge of the jungle, we read in the literature of the age—any age—may begin just outside the living room door. Its fecund odor sweeps across the room, passing like the trade winds between my easy chair and the TV set, then curling gently down over the rocky plain of the Scrabble board, until the children look up aghast. "Daddy!" they cry. They have no understanding of what happens to one's stomach at my age. Nor do I. Enough to have to live with it. After all these years they are as bad as I: still unaccustomed to the flatulent parent ensconced with a supply of beer and potato chips before the picture of a distant and insignificant baseball game—a minor and late-season encounter, of no import to the final standings, in the "other" league. But this time they are wrong. The game—although even the umpires don't know it yet and so designate it merely as a delay—has been rained out in the bottom of the third (no score, two out, man on second, two-ball–no-strike count on batter). The other commercial stations show the great movies of my own childhood: *Thunderhead, Son of Flicka; The Purple Heart; Destry Rides Again.* I have tuned to the educational station, arriving in the midst of a program on pre-Columbian explorations of the New World. A priest, standing before a blowup of an ancient but, I can see, not wholly inaccurate map of the North Atlantic, is extolling the seamanship and cartography of the Irish. The Irish!

His head remains, as he talks, directly in front of the spot where Greenland ought to be on the map, if Greenland is on this map. Neither Marco Polo nor Columbus nor, for that matter, any traveler whom I personally have known was ever loathe to embellish his journey to good effect. With pity and terror, according to formula. But not too much. The Irish priest-scholar is replaced by the more usual tall, bearded Scandinavian, who has his own map, a modern one, upon which Sweden, Iceland, Newfoundland, New York, and the Great Lakes are all carefully labeled. On the floor, in spite of the interruption, the youngest child has just managed, with the help of several existing letters, to fit the word QUOTIDIAN into the upper right-hand corner, thereby claiming a double triple word score that would, if allowed, set a family record, and setting into motion a bitter argument that will last far into the evening and may, for all I know, remain unsettled to this day. And they are, in the meantime, quite wrong. It was not I that we smelled, this time.

But how am I to explain that to them? Already this, the most significant event of their eleventh, thirteenth, and fourteenth years, respectively, is of no interest to them. Were I to come vocally to my own defense, they would merely look at me in silence, exchange glances, and return to their bickering. They have, there, a tight, familiar circle. Who dares to shatter it? Coleridge, we all know, was jarred from his dream of a sacred river whose circular flow enclosed a perfectly self-contained world by a simple, unexpected pull at the doorbell. Was there no one who could have answered it for him, kept one world at bay for just a few more stanzas of another world that he was never again able to return to? Columbus, dreaming of the circumnavigation of the globe via the westward route to the Indies, woke up one day to find himself lost and adrift in the Caribbean archipelago. With the smell of the spice islands in his nostrils he was only able, after that, to navigate into mismanagement, enslavement, delusion, ignominy, shipwreck, and death. What do we learn from history? The greatest men in the world can't hold a course: Moses, Alexander, Socrates, Copernicus. The rank flatulence of reality seeps through the narrowest cracks. Who wants to open the door to that?

Me, I'm sorry to say. I do. Why? Because it's too warm on this mid-September afternoon to sit in the house with all the doors and windows closed. Because I thought I heard a car in the driveway, perhaps my wife coming home from work early, her imitation jaguar coat draped over her arm. Isn't it time for the evening paper to be delivered? The truth is, I want to know what that smell is, and I want it known, in here, for what it is. Out there. I rise up in front of the TV set, abandon the English moderator in the midst of his cautious summing up, cross the living room in my stockinged feet, and fling open the front door. The screen door is still in place, though it's time to begin thinking of putting up the storm doors and windows. There is no newspaper, no wife, no cool breeze to air out the stuffy house. Only a heavy, meaty smell, hanging, for a moment, like a brocade curtain in the doorway, and then, with the slightest movement, perhaps merely the breeze stirred by my own motion, crumbling slowly inward. Of the children who should be attending to its entrance, one has already departed for the rear of the house, leaving an echo of slammed doors behind, another burrows away into the couch, rule book in one hand and dictionary in the other, while the third sits rigidly erect in the center of the room, eyes clenched shut, hands over ears. A new program is just getting underway on the educational station, Beginning Spanish: Useful Phrases for Travelers. "This smell," I announce, "is really incredible." No one pays any attention to anything.

Gingerly, being shoeless, I step outside onto the concrete walk. Never, never, have I smelled anything like this! And yet I don't want to say that it's a "bad" smell. We read in Captain John Smith's *Diary* of the "offensive odour of these unclene salvages," and yet the next entry reflects his undaunted desire to "traffick" with them. Nor did the Indians, for their part, remain aloof, though we know they referred to Jamestown as the "village-of-the-stinking-houses." The least I expected was to find my neighbors gathered on their front steps. Didn't they all rush forth like that, instead of into the safety of the southwest corners of their basements, when the tornado warning sirens sounded? And wasn't this a disaster of at least equal proportions? What would become of property values if a smell such as this became a permanent fixture in the neighborhood? We might become used to it, of course, might even affirm to each other after a while that we actually enjoyed it, or identify it to outsiders as essential to the "special quality" of our neighborhood; but who, given its presence, would deliberately buy a house, move in here, even at depreciated prices? And who, for that matter, would want to live with people who could accept such a smell as a normal part of their lives?

But except for a child hurtling down the sloping sidewalk on his tricycle, head hunched forward over the handlebars, the street is deserted. The voice of antagonism I can hear rising from within the depths of my own house, ignorant of the oppressive smell that envelops its chambered shell as it envelops all these other, silent, ones about me. For days the Norsemen under Bjarni Herjolfsson drifted soundlessly in dense fog off the Newfoundland banks, blanketed by the rich smells of a land they could not find their way to. What of those tales of Portuguese traders finding their way to Ceylon by following its wind-borne fragrances? Here, however, not a breeze stirs. The smell coagulates upon the neighborhood like an ancient stew, muffling the ragged purr of the white Ford that swings into my driveway. My wife leaves it there, cuts across the dry, uncut grass of the lawn toward me, coat draped over her shoulders in spite of the muggy atmosphere. "Well?" I say to her. "Well?" she says, no doubt surprised to find me out there. "The smell," I say, "what about the smell?" "Smell," she says, lifting her nose and sniffing about her, "What smell?"

ii

There are various things that, in the course of time, I may or may not come to know about this smell. I may, for example, come to know the language and literature of this smell. Through it I may come to grasp the intentional mode of transitive verbs: *e.g.*, "to smell." In some exotic foreign language there is perhaps a far more precise terminology which deals with "smell" in the same detailed fashion in which the language of the Eskimos deals with "snow." Think of all the possible relevant passages in the *Encyclopedia Britannica* alone. What of its use by writers throughout the ages? By Hakluyt and Swift and Smollett? By John Donne and Edgar Rice Burroughs and the

Gnostics? Who knows what discoveries may be embraced or denied by critical commentaries upon this very word?

Perhaps I shall also come to know of the intricate relationship between this smell and its environment. Of changes in its texture and intensity in accordance with shifts in temperature and/or humidity. Of a curious, ancient chart for this relationship, in the shape of a calabash. Of a quest for the unvarying, perfect combination of temperature and humidity. Of its impossibility.

There are also numerous miscellaneous things which I may or may not come to know about this smell. The myth of species distinction, for example. Or that perfumes, instead of obliterating, it, are, by its presence, themselves rendered . . . rancid. How plants are affected by it. The science of its "flow" or direction. Its topological, medical, allomorphic, hermeneutical, sociopathic, political, mutagenic, aesthetic, nosological, anthropometric, holographic, epistemological, literary, and centristic implications. Its "meat and potatoes" nature.

And perhaps I shall come to know nothing, nothing at all. I shall only be left with the smell. And myself.

iii

Certain birds, which cross the Himalayas twice yearly in their migrations between Russia and India, become more familiar to me than my own neighbors. Can you imagine that: the Himalayas! Storm-swept, five miles high, perpetual snows, how do they do it? Do they send scouts ahead to seek out the passes and protected mountain valleys? Do the strong up-drafts off the Gangetic plain carry the odors of the South up through the mountain passes, creating fragrant skyways to guide them home? These are not the rich odors of the Indies that Columbus hoped to track around the world. These are the odors of life and death.

"Smell or die," I announce at the dinner table. My wife looks up at me, fork poised in midair, more surprised, I suspect, at the harshness of my tone than at the sadism of the statement. The children, swamped in the heavy odors of boeuf bourguignon, steeped in the richness of its burgundy scent, do not even look up from their eating. The sharp cinnamon breath of the spice cake still in the oven edges in from the kitchen. From the salad bowl, bleu cheese and tarragon vinegar cleave the air with their linked strength. All this is an act of memory, the imaginative re-creation of a desperate man. I smell only one smell. The boeuf bourguignon hath lost its savor. Small birds are already winging south at incredible altitudes, only a dim scent of the future to guide them. So enveloped am I in this one smell that I know not which way to turn. Even the jasmine incense smoldering on the mantelpiece fails to penetrate; I cannot remember what its once oppressive and delightful odor was "like." If I were sitting on one of those rotating secretarial chairs or lunch counter stools, I would spin and spin before these eaters and insensate smellers. "Smell *and* die," I amend. My wife smiles—more, I suspect, at my chastened tone than at my masochistic message—then lowers her fork to her plate and resumes eating.

But I cannot. I don't want to say that there is something of putrefaction to the smell, but at the same time I cannot find in it anything . . . healthy. That's not altogether true. I detect within it something like a trace of ripe peaches, that sweet, and yet, at the same time, something dully reminiscent of my days in the chemistry lab. No, that's all wrong, there are no traces of "other things" within the smell itself, none. It is pure, solid, dominant, a great lava flow of itself, impenetrable as that Torrid Zone was said to be which early explorers feared to approach too closely lest they actually be roasted to death. Substantially *there.* As one approached its edges, human flesh turned darker. Signs for all to comprehend. Dimension, mass, density. Can these children, who, for a moment at least, experienced it there with me, at first, have already forgotten? "Don't you remember the smell?" I demand of them, leaning forward across my still-clean dinner plate. The room is silent, their own plates are almost emptied now. They eat so well. They look back at me with utter lack of comprehension. Can they have adapted to it so swiftly that they no longer notice its presence? If they can, why can't I? When they recoiled from its edges, was I already caught in its center? I'm starving, but even the water seems thick with it, coating the inside of my mouth as I drink. How can they fail to observe something of such weight, such near opacity? Or are they merely trying to be protective, to save face? Whose then? Mine? The nerve of them! Don't they understand that this has to do with all of us, with the whole house, the whole neighborhood, perhaps the whole world, not just me? "You damn fools," I splutter at them, "that smell wasn't what you think!" But they merely look embarrassed and begin to clear the table noisily, disappearing into the kitchen with the dishes.

iv

Now that the children are gone once again—to bed this time—and my wife has plunged into the odorless ideas of her book and my hunger has been assuaged not by food but by time, the moment arrives to face the question squarely: What do I smell? It's well past time, in fact. The umpire's delay is long since an officially rained-out game. Dawn on the far side of the globe sends the migratory flock into the air once again, dooming many of its individuals in the quest for the passage south over those enormous mountains. Columbus has died still believing he tracked the scent of the Indies into the true East. And the neighbors, I see from my living room window, are blinking out their lights one by one, all unawares.

After dinner I prowled the neighborhood, nostrils aquiver, hoping to follow its spoor among them where they placidly grazed on their lawns in the warm, bug-free autumn evening. They rustled nervously at my approach, unaccustomed to my presence among them. I stayed on the walk as the males came cautiously toward me, leaning slightly forward from the waist, maneuvering their mates and young to a position of safety behind them. Once upon a time I had a rather large dog who, as he grew old and bloated, constantly filled the house with the insufferable odors of his flatulence. For many years, then, I was in the habit of taking him for frequent walks, to air both the dog and the house. Behind him on the leash, I found that he served as my *carte d'identite*. Females and children, leaving their males far behind, came bounding fearlessly over the lawns to fondle him and talk to me. He's dead now, but that's another story. In still younger days I remember always carrying the invitation with me on the evening of the party, lest my right to be present be considered suspect. Now they moved restlessly from side to side before me as I stood alone and dogless in their presence, unable to articulate my mission. They were, I thought, altogether capable of suddenly turning their backs upon me, spewing their feces behind them to lighten themselves for flight, and bolting for the safety of their open doorways. The edgy odor of fear—that tell-tale prelude to the "flight reaction"—I knew already. *That* wasn't what I smelled.

And yet, without my introducing the subject, they—the men who took their stands before me, nervously shuffling their feet, pawing the ground—spoke one and all of smells. They were pleased with how fine the air smelled now, thanks to a recent ordinance prohibiting open incineration of garbage. They were pleased that the scent of fall was in the air. They had brought back from a summer trip to the seaside the very smell of salt air. They looked forward to the odor of leaves burning on October afternoons. They smelled, their words seemed meant to assure me, both well and good.

And what, meanwhile, did *I* smell? I sat by myself on the front steps as the final glow of evening faded from the sky, and, with the descending chill, this trenchant odor reached, though remaining unchanged, a new level of sharpness. When those men crinkled their noses while they spoke to me of smells remembered or anticipated, was it merely a facial tic, the body's assent to the conversation? Or was it, in fact, the body's giveaway, an admission that the words were mere bravado? Or was it a silent hint directed at me? But I bathed as often as anyone else, changed my clothes as frequently, used the same deodorants, soothed my gassy bowels with antacid tablets at home and restrained them abroad. Besides, I know the odor—the odors—of the human body, and this was not it, not any of them. What was it then? It was almost dark. I was close to shivering in the chill. I was, except for this omnipresent smell, quite alone. Naturally my responses tended toward the pretentious. Even the moon, I saw, was affected, appearing, though it was full and the night was clear and it should have shone with harvest brilliance, behind a lackluster haze. Could it be, I wondered, the smell of sin? The stench of corruption? The taint of mortality? Nothing could be stronger than that, could it? But what did I imagine: that in the middle of this particular day I, among all men, had suddenly received the gift of clairolfacience? Who needed it? Even with a heavy cold, not one iota of *this* smell could I have escaped. Standing up in the darkness, expelling the accumulated gases of the evening, I could almost handle it, it was that real. And if I could have gotten my hands on it, I think I would have choked it, it was that alive. As it was, I merely stood with it draped over my head and shoulders like a mantle for a moment before going indoors, while my own foul aroma drifted up about me. That too was real. And all too lively.

In the living room the children are grouped around the tidy flame of the TV set, their running battle over the afternoon's Scrabble game erupting at each commercial break, going abruptly silent as their program, a spy story set in the Middle East, resumes. My wife, who would gladly have accompanied me on my after dinner excursion, looks up from her book, her expression precariously balanced between amusement and concern. Although the smell—not my smell, *the* smell—is almost as dense in here as it was outside, the straight, classic lines of her nose remain motionless, attesting to her innocence. On the TV set the two American spies lie bound and unconscious in a shabby warehouse while their mysteriously robed captors empty cannisters of gasoline across the floor and set the spilled liquid alight. Soon they will awake to the acrid smell of smoke. How will they manage their escape this time? The flight of their foreign tormentors is interrupted by a commercial for a new, remarkably long-lasting deodorant: "Even a plunge in the salty Atlantic leaves you still protected!" My wife is reading the latest of those books which attempt to explain the human phenomenon in terms of some central metaphor: game, structure, language, organism. *Homo incipiens*: man always about to be. The bikini-clad girl in the commercial leaps from the waves, arms upraised, spraying water in all directions, mimicking those Polynesian girls who splashed eagerly across the bay to throw themselves upon the men of Captain

Cook's crew. Who'll rub me in cocoanut oil? Stuff my nostrils with cloves and cinnamon? Season the evening air with a shower of gardenias?

When the ten o'clock news comes on we all turn to it in silent expectation. Will I be proven right after all? Has a tank car full of chemicals derailed and overturned, releasing its exotic contents into our atmosphere? Has an oil refinery exploded, filling the air with its coarse fumes? Has a foreign trade delegation descended heavily upon us with the goods and aromas of its native land? Is it the river? Factories? Vegetation? *What* do I smell? We are still waiting in silence when the weatherman maps out his high-pressure areas and the sports announcer catalogs the rained-out games in other parts of the country.

v

Midnight. Family sleeps. Earth revolves. What may I, or may I not, come to know? Birds, dogs, neighbors, books, great explorers . . . all fade. Only the jungle breathes, exudes. A continent forcing its presence outward upon the seas. The smell hovers, purer, more lucid, than ever. Not only the smell. I am here with it. Look at me, smell me. Impossible. Look me up in a book then. Here I am, an odorless, invisible phenomenon. Is that me? Try the commentaries. An island, at the very least, in my own imagination, I am doing the best I can to outfit an exploratory cruise. Who'll join me? Tomorrow the skies will clear, all the scheduled games will be played. I have no "proof" of anything. On the contrary, the evidence is all against me. In their sleep the children chuckle at the scent of my folly, the neighbors dream this house and lot into a park where they can walk their dogs. At last I begin to understand Columbus' difficulties. The best I can expect is a wormy vessel and a rebellious crew. He had only himself to rely on. If the prisons were opened to staff my expedition, who would come forth? Maybe only this one sleeper here who remembers how I could identify the children by their smells alone. Blind as a bat, I could still tell who was sneaking up behind me before I turned around and put my glasses on. But we outgrow our smelling. On the edges where we come to dwell we are no longer aware of our centers.

Presence: I smell *something*. That's what I've been trying to say all along. And my presence: *I* smell something. Who said that? Alone, in the night, alerted to its presence: I can almost feel the earth revolving beneath me, the light waiting in the distance, the darkness beyond that. You don't just smell: you smell *something*. See. Hear. Those things *are*. Taste. Touch. Specific themselves, they awaken the specific in me. Feel. Talk to. Wake up! I have a name, not given yet. The children have names. The neighbors. The dogs. What I have learned so far, after dark, in the course of time, alone with this smell, in the night, alive. To be translated into the specific. All smells are real smells, in the smelling. Out of that comes something, rather than nothing. Making me real. I smell this, taste that, imagine the other. Presence to presence. It's not so unbearable as I first thought. Even in here. Together we take our place in the world. No need for verification by the news or the neighbors. We are on the way. We sail at dawn, regardless of the weather, knowing only a few bookish things about navigation, in a vessel shaped like . . . something not quite suited for the open seas. No matter. Tomorrow, under partly cloud skies, Kansas City vs. Cleveland, not televised. Monopoly instead of scrabble: my token, if I am allowed to play, the ship. Flatulence not to be spoken of. Other smells not acknowledged, as usual. Although the children know what *they* smelled—when they smelled it. It was me after all—of course!—if only for a moment and not as they thought. Or is it: merely not as I thought they thought? No wonder they were embarrassed. I'll wake them and tell them: "Never forget." Or does everyone else know and remember these things already? Birds shuffling in their sleep in the aromatic winds of the Himalayan foothills. Mapless explorers attuned to the entire presence of the worlds they navigate. Charts to come after: "Here in the night we were all awakened when the wind shifted to due west and brought the smell of the forest to us, and at dawn did sight what we believed to be the mainland, at less than a league's distance." Sitting up naked in bed in the presence of all this in the middle of the night—any night—I am, I realize, my own *carte d'identite*.

The Discovery of America

Amerigo Vespucci, one of the truly remarkable figures of the Age of Exploration, a man you studied at least twice, perhaps even three times, when you "did" the explorers in grade school and junior high, the man, in fact, for whom your own country is named: what do you really know about him?

Choose one:

(a)   Commander of a Portuguese expedition, he ignored the Papal division of New World lands between Spain and Portugal, discovered Rio de Janeiro Bay, and explored the South American coast at least as far south as the River Plate.

(b)   Son of an Italian notary, he rose swiftly to a position of power with the Medicis and played, on their behalf, both behind the scenes and as an explorer himself, a significant role in the era of discovery.

(c)   As navigator of a Spanish expedition under Ojeda, he recklessly left the main body of the exploratory fleet, sailed on his own as far as Cape Consolacion, sighted the mouth of the Orinoco, and managed to rejoin his commander in Española (Haiti) in time for the confrontation that led to the downfall of Columbus.

(d)   All of the above.

(e)   None of the above.

Or would you like to select parts of several of the above—with, perhaps, various additions and deletions of your own: to make up the Amerigo of your imagination? He lived, after all—and died—

49

over four hundred and fifty years ago; as with most of his contem-
poraries, the little we know of him—though indeed, we know more
about him than about most of the others—leaves us a portrait somewhat blurred by distance. Nor has the glare of historical research and
biographical spotlighting done more, in the end, than to wash out
even many of those details that seemed, at one time, to be marked
with clear, sharp edges.

Quelando, for example, as might be expected not only of a
nineteenth-century biographer in the romantic tradition but as an
Hispanicist as well, raised him to a level of heroism unmatched before
or after, so that it has often been said that the pinnacle of Vespucci's
career was achieved only in 1848. Here, as nowhere else, are we
given, in a finely wrought drama heightened by the author's attempts
to re-create crucial conversations in his protagonist's rise to fame,
climactic meetings with the other great figures of his time, a sense of
the fearless and intrepid seafarer, knowledgeable not only in the ways
of the earth and its elements but the ways of men as well, gifted with
a clear-sightedness that far surpassed Columbus' murky, visionary
approach to exploration, a man of noble mein and lofty ideals who
truly deserved to have continents named after him.

Wheelwright, however, writing half a century or more later and
out of his own period's struggle to achieve a balanaced view of its
origins, places Vespucci dead center among a broad constellation of
daring men—not just the Spanish, Portuguese, and Italian, but
Dutch and English as well, even the French—each of whom was
beset by problems but each of whom made his own unique and
necessary contribution to the opening up of the Western Hemisphere. And Schwartzkopf, on the other hand, viewing this character—for such time makes him, does it not, a character rather than a
person?—not only in the light of more recent historical evidence but
also with the more cynical gaze that has become the scholarly hall-
mark of this, our own time, denigrates him to a mere fourth-rate
talent; a shallow imitator attempting to walk in the giant footsteps of
Columbus; a small-time promoter who knew a good thing when he

saw it but had neither the bravery nor the intelligence that swept others of his age to great accomplishments; a moderate success only at the sort of court intrigue through which he might secure a safe and profitable post—preferably at home, where he could reap the benefits while other risked their lives on dangerous seas and in unknown lands.

Not one of those, of course, is the Amerigo Vespucci of our childhood, he whose dotted red line followed Columbus' looping black ones across the blue mid-Atlantic in our fifth-grade social studies book; he whose name we affixed in the proper blank space following the question, "After what great explorer was America named?"; he who was, in spite of that glowing mark of recognition, given only a single line in the text, and in the eighth grade shared a paragraph with Cortez and Balboa. Nope, not him.

But at a distance of almost five centuries, who could hope to keep a steady eye on things? First you squint and peer across the ages like a chimpanzee imitating a human frown, looking at the exact spot where your teacher is pointing. And if you see only a dull haze there, with a faint glimmer suggesting movement of some sort, nonetheless you tell her, when she asks, that what you see there is just what she told you you'd see there. Perhaps the second or third time, you actually do see what you're supposed to see. What else? Only much later, perhaps, when no one cares whether you look or not—when, maybe, no one really wants you to look any longer—you begin to wonder what it was that was really there after all. You try to remember how it was done, to find the right direction. You look, you squint, you hunch down and shade your eyes with your hands.

"Amerigo?"

Something moves out there. Your eyes blur. You blink them clear.

"Amerigo Vespucci?"

You have to make up your mind whether it's really worth all this effort. Because what you see out there is what's there.

"Who is it? Really."

I too have traveled, though for myself, I was never quite sure what I was looking for. Inheritor of the great tradition of *On The Road*, I nonetheless managed to remain in one place for the first three decades of my life. Was it because, as I was told, I had my "roots" there? In the same way that Van Daam, in his volume on the fifteenth century, says that all the explorers were "rooted" in the Renaissance? And yet he refutes himself, showing how, one by one, the first strong wind that came along (whatever it was: gold, fame, adventure, curiosity) carried each of them immediately off. Tumbleweeds all, rootless as I myself proved when, for the first time *ever*, something interesting blew my way. An offer of a job.

That the offer itself was merely a light breeze—so slight, in fact, that I shall here declare it unworthy of mention—and that it soon faded away, leaving me totally becalmed, is only fuller evidence of how rootless I indeed was, for with not so much as a whisper to fill my sails—it wasn't much of a job at all, the truth is that I was more disappointed in them than they in me—I still continued merrily on my way. I found myself in Seattle, a lovely city whose entire population consisted of people who had come from somewhere else. Perhaps the main lure of that wispy offer was the opportunity it represented to get the farthest I could from where I was and still remain in the adjacent forty-eight. But having bumped up against the western edges, why stop there, when still other directions were open, south for example? I found myself in Mexico, a lovely country vibrant with the heat of many comings and goings. On the horizon, the seductive shimmer of distances. Back in the States, I found myself in a lovely southern town, full of people who had never been anywhere else. One of the few respectable cities in the world not built on water of any sort. And not a hundred miles from my starting point.

I have looked on the maps and observed the remarkable shapes—the circles, the ellipses, the figure eights—transcribed thereon by the voyages of the great explorers. And then I see on the map that my own journey has been more or less ovoid in shape. An egg, set big end up, with a crack in the upper right shoulder, where the end has failed to come together with the beginning:

Around the perimeter of that figure I have traveled with an increasingly large entourage, all of us gaining, by stages, a gradual awareness of what lies in the center of it: who is really there. We have me surrounded at last, except for that one small gap already noted. Through it. . . .

Through it what? I leak away? I escape?

I emerge.

It is noon, but frighteningly dark. Amerigo Vespucci sits, cross-legged on the empty deck, in the crucial chapter of the Jones volume in the Lives of Great Men series, riding out a sudden storm that has descended almost as soon as he and his comrades have turned their backs on the western lands and set out for home. It is a sort of storm that Vespucci and his companions have never seen before, for which they have no name except terror. The sailors huddle below, their moans blotted out by the wind. Even Ojeda keeps to his cabin; and only Vespucci, who has just left that foul-smelling den, knows just how sick the commander really is. Columbus, he also knows, is reported to be a fine sailor, is said never to have been sick at sea. Already Vespucci knows that this is only because there is no weather for Columbus except what blows inside his own head. Vespucci himself is not so fine a sailor by any means.

As the ship, flying one solitary sail, already torn, rides out enormous waves, he is fully aware of the nausea that hangs over him, the waves that tower above the mast and higher still, the great emptiness beneath. Nonetheless, he is preoccupied with composing, in his mind, the letter to his employers that he will encode and dispatch at the earliest possible moment after his arrival. Behind him, though they are only hours out, the island is wholly obscured by the storm; were it not for the violence with which the winds drive from that very direction, they would no doubt be heading back, at this very moment, to the safety of its harbor. In Vespucci's mind, however, the island remains visible with an incredible clarity. The letter, with its cautious superlatives, is almost completed. No longer can the heavy sheets of rain be distinguished from the great seas which break across the deck. The words "home," "storm," "sea," "danger" become rapidly water-soaked, blur and fade. He signs his name, "Amerigo Vespucci," with a flourish. He is already on his way back.

iii

The last time I saw Amerigo Vespucci face-to-face was in Lexington, Kentucky, in the rare book room of the university library. There, in an eighteenth–century reproduction of Waldseemuller's 1507 map of the world, an ancient likeness of Ptolemy graced the hemisphere containing the Old World, but his was the portrait, the handsome Roman profile of Amerigo Vespucci, that emblazoned the hemisphere of the New World. The map may have left much to be desired, but the figure in the portrait made it perfectly clear that all this was his. Like a spider he had circled the Atlantic, spinning a delicate web across the sea, and now he perched, at last, on the edge, where he could sense the vibrations in each and every strand. No one moved without consulting him, no one returned without reporting to him. Columbus, raving of Cathay and his right to the governorship of the Indies, was dead, whereas Vespucci had achieved a position that knotted together the strands of his Portuguese, Spanish, and Italian enterprises and, save for those latecomers the Dutch and English, virtually put him in charge of the opening up of the New World.

What, I had to wonder, perched along the edge of a dusty desk in a stifling, windowless room, peering at the book lying open on my lap, had his true orders been? To keep a watchful eye on the Jew Columbus? To test the real limits of Spanish and Portuguese power in the

Western Hemisphere? To gain the confidence of governments that would enable him to work his way into a seat of knowledge and influence from which he could well advise his real employers? For that was what he finally did, gaining, in spite of his dubious reports on and actions in the New World, so stable a reputation as a scrupulous man and a brilliant navigator that he was at last recalled to Spain, appointed to the Commercial House for the West Indies, and, finally, made *piloto mayor*, chief navigator, a position that empowered him to examine and license all pilots embarking on voyages of exploration, to prepare maps of newly discovered lands and the routes for reaching them, and to interpret and coordinate the continuing stream of valuable information that the explorers were required to furnish.

Did he, I wondered, not a two-hour drive myself, and that in an air-conditioned car, from closing the circuit of my own journeying, *did he*, I wondered, still take his orders, *then*, from the Medici? Or did he, in those long ellipses his ships described upon the unpredictable Atlantic, discover something more about who was in the center of those voyages than he had originally been contracted for? What of this *man*, I wondered, this solid-looking middle-aged man whose profiled gaze on the page before me incorporated both the Americas? Why, in his mid-fifties, did he suddenly decide to take up Spanish citizenship? Who was this historical stranger who peeled back the illusions of his time to reveal the old lands of the East as the New World of the West, who left us a name from which it appears we shall never escape and, though he did not bargain like Columbus for 10 percent of the gross and a family title in perpetuity, left his wife Maria with a generous pension, provided by the Spanish government in recognition of his great contribution? What of *him*?

In a Seattle bar tucked away under the edge of the bridge that spans the Union Canal and called, I have no doubt, though I don't remember having ever seen the name posted anywhere, the Bridge Café, I discussed, with a fellow worker, over watery dark beer, the question of roots. His, not mine.

"If I ever had them," I told him, "I've cut them off, they're gone.

Thirty years of roots is enough to strangle on. Who needs *roots*? If you want some, you can have mine."

He didn't want my roots, of course, he wanted his own. Seattle, with its mild weather and perpetual rains, was green all year round. On its steep hillsides gardens flowered among the rocks, tended or not. Strangers from the most distant parts of the country met here and merged; families blossomed from them. A mere passerby who found a certain relief even in riding the ferry boats aimlessly about Puget Sound, I found the whole process vaguely suspect.

"Is it possible," I inquired of this friend, whose doubly mixed parentage left open to him, still, the choice of whether to be Jew or Protestant, American or Canadian, "to really 'put down' roots? Aren't roots what you grow *from* rather than to ?"

When he was finished with his lecture on taking cuttings from house-plants, and the discursion on the rooting of ivies in water or vermiculite, and had begun to muse, over the empty pitcher of beer, about the fertile growth potential of residency in the United States watered by Canadian citizenship, I found it necessary to object that we had had enough, that the analogy had become uselessly complicated.

"Besides," I pointed out, "all analogies are false analogies."

"There have been some very interesting comparisons between the lives of certain men," he said, cutting my objection adrift with a little smile. "Some have been known to structure their lives on the analogy of prior models."

The pitcher of beer still sat empty on the table before us. From the way he had pushed his chair back from the table, angled it toward me, and planted his feet firmly on the floor between us, I could tell he had just begun. Newcomers drifted in through the doorway, pausing to shake the rain from their clothing and let their eyes adjust to the darkness. The vast, dim interior of the Bridge Café began to fill up with sullen examples.

In a living room in one of the great cities of the Ohio Valley I met, recumbent among the bric-a-brac of nations—ivory elephants, teak end tables, flamingoes carved from bone, cloisonné cigarette boxes—the "world traveler." He told me, at some length, how he went to "New York" to see the "Empire State Building" and, after that, to "Acapulco" to see the "ocean" and then, the following year, to "Japan" to see the "Japanese," including a stopover, on his return, in "Hawaii" to see a "volcano." He was, he said, an avid traveler who never tired of such opportunities to see "the world" and was always eager, when he returned, to tell his friends about "Tel Aviv," the "Eiffel Tower," or "camels." With rare exceptions, he claimed, his trips always went smoothly throughout. The "weather" was always perfect. Only occasionally was he annoyed when the people of some "foreign country" failed to try hard enough to understand him, when a ticket agent confessed that the "flight" on which he had been scheduled was oversold, or when he was overcharged for a "meal." But such occurrences never bothered him for long, for he knew that they did the same things to you in "Las Vegas" and "Miami Beach" as in "Tangiers" or "Hong Kong." He had long since learned to adopt a philosophical attitude toward "events." What he said was, "Things work out for the best," and nothing that had ever "happened" or that anyone had ever "said," whether in "Cincinnati" or in "Bangkok," had ever shaken his faith in that statement.

The first time I met Amerigo Vespucci was on the one occasion of my venturing into the center of that ovoid already described—a ruthless day and night dash westward across the August-roasted flatlands of Indiana, Illinois, Missouri, Kansas, and eastern Colorado in a black and white air-conditioned Chrysler: into the eastern Rockies. On the road up Pikes Peak I skidded past one of those little roadside shrines, the kind that, though rarely seen in the United States, border all the highways of Mexico yet seem always unvisited by tourists or anyone else. What did I see this time, out of the corner of my eye, up there just above the timberline? I wasn't sure, but I wanted to stop, all the same. It was a full mile before I found a graveled turnaround where I could leave the car off the road and walk back down. Almost everyone who passed offered me a ride in one direction or the other. "Something wrong with your car?" No.

Yes. There was no doubt about it. The shrine was unmarked, as they always are—one is expected to *know* one's saints—but the little statue in it was unmistakable. I knelt down before it, in the drainage ditch by the side of the road. A plaster niche, resting back against the solid, soaring granite of the mountainside, but molded, if my eyes didn't deceive me, rather vaguely in the shape of a seashell. Now the cars that passed me no longer stopped but only slowed, while their occupants pointed. Children poked their heads out of windows. The "pilgrim" turned and looked back at them over his shoulder. Did he, in his crisp blue sport shirt, look like a dedicated worshipper who had just trudged to the twelve-thousand-foot level (we were *that* near the top)? Up here, perhaps, they were willing to take most anything for granted. A discovery was a discovery, always worth pointing at, like Cripple Creek somewhere down below us.

Inside the weathered, crumbling plaster shell, paint peeling—he was almost stripped down to pale white flesh—Amerigo also pointed. Seated on a globe, the great bulge of South America just slipping out from beneath his left thigh and a cluster of navigational instruments firmly grasped in his left hand, his right arm pointed straight out, toward me. Or, when I scooted aside, at the horizon. What did he see? Unlike Columbus, who died still believing—or still trying to convince himself—that he had landed on the islands off the east coast of the Asian mainland, Vespucci, after his second voyage—or at least after his final voyage, however many it was he actually took—realized that he had come upon a "new world." Was *that* his real discovery? What did he point at now? I followed the direction of the arm. There was nothing there. Only the emptiness between mountains. It was Amerigo all right.

When I had climbed back at last to my car, it wouldn't start. Vapor lock, I was assured by the first of many passing motorists who stopped to offer their assistance. This disgnosis was confirmed by all. Just wait, they instructed. I waited, evening approached, the skies began to run through their changes of color, every bit as beautiful and spacious as claimed, but the car still refused to start. It's always vapor lock up here, I was assured, but nonetheless with some help I got the car turned around and pointed downhill, not realizing until it started to roll silently ahead that, well equipped as it was, without the motor running I had no power for the power steering, no power for the power brakes. O Amerigo, what have you done to me upon these precipices!

At a roadside turnoff high in the Sierras south of Mexico City, south even of Cuernavaca and Oaxaca, in arid, desolate country where not a cow or a goat had strayed across the road in hours, and hardly a village had been seen beside it, we parked and dropped the tailgate of our station wagon to prepare a picnic lunch. We opened the ham and rolls bought earlier in the morning; the children returned from their trips behind some nearby boulders to cluster around us; a man in immaculate white clothing, leading a burro, came walking around a bend in the highway. Friendly tourists all, we waved, he crossed over to our side of the road, the children clutched sandwiches in one hand and petted his animal with the other, we invited him, in our rudimentary Spanish, to eat with us, but he politely refused. He seemed far more interested in the car than in us or in our food, and examined its dusty blue length quite thoroughly before turning at last to us.

"Americano?" he asked. He was friendly and with an unladen burro obviously had nothing to sell, but as I stuffed the last bite of sandwich into my mouth and wiped my mayonnaise-smeared fingers on my pants, I wondered about that word he had chosen to use and whether it wasn't, here and now, time to do something about it.

"No," I answered him, in the best Spanish I could muster, "no soy Americano solamente."

"No Americano?" he said, puzzled. Even my family, generally prompted by good manners to ignore my struggles with foreign languages, looked around at me in rather quizzical fashion.

"Yo soy *norte* Americano," I explained. No one moved.

"Yo soy un hombre de los Estados Unidos," I continued, after a brief pause.

"Yo soy un gringo," I added, thinking to make a joke, but he didn't even smile.

"Y usted es un Mexicano," I concluded, "pero los dos son Amer-
icanos." I was a gringo all right, there wasn't anything I could do
about that, There, the point had been made. But I wasn't one of your
greedy gringos, I didn't want all the Americas for myself.

"Usted es Americano," he said, and walked away, burro in tow.

iv

We met once more, Vespucci and I, as prearranged, in a drab tavern
on lower Vine Street in Cincinnati. It is a place where neither of us
belongs or feels safe, but where we can both be certain of remaining
unrecognized. Except for us, the meager early afternoon crowd con-
sists entirely of lean, hard-looking, poorly dressed men, migrants
from the hills of West Virginia and eastern Kentucky, who talk, in low
voices, either of going on to Chicago and Detroit or of returning to
the impoverished creeks and hollows that they have just left. Over
the harsh angularities of their dialect, their eyes constantly roam to
the booth near the door where we sit, Vespucci and I, in our simple
but obviously "good" clothes.

Vespucci is highly nervous. He plays with the saltshaker, spins
the filthy glass ashtray, expresses his fear that Portuguese agents are
after him, on orders to punish him for defecting back to Spain after
the great expense Portugal has gone to in financing his last expedition. What do they mean by *punish*? Has he really done any harm to
anyone? Would they be satisfied by having him return to sail under
the Portuguese flag once again? Was it not in the service of the king
of Portugal that he first opened the eyes of the world to what was
really out there? What does he care whose flag he sails under, whose
money is behind a voyage? Is it not discovery alone that counts?

Even the bartender has paused, in his wiping of glasses, to stare
open-mouthed at this sudden outburst, though in all probability he
has not understood a single word of Vespucci's rapid-fire mono-
logue. He and his other customers turn back to their own affairs as I
break in to explain, calmly and slowly, how I myself have now finally
completed the last unfinished leg of my own circular journey. I say

"circular" because I fear that in his agitated state he will not have the patience to listen to a more elaborate explanation of the sort of figure I think I have been mapping out for myself. With a last brief lurch, I am right back where I started, I tell him. He can hardly sit still any longer. There are private letters, letters which he wrote to the Medici—"for their eyes only"—which, it now appears, have fallen into the wrong hands. Was it before or after their delivery? One way or another, the effects on his reputation are apt to be severe, are they not? What will people think of him, in years to come? He only wanted to do what was right, isn't that so? Isn't that what he wanted?

I put my hand on his. How can I stop here? I ask him. I don't even want to be seen here, that's why we agreed to meet in a place like this, where I couldn't be brought to a halt by cries of recognition but could complete my round and keep on going, just one more major journey that could carry me well on beyond where I started. He jerks his hand away from me, not sure he even wants to hear talk of another voyage. Where? Why? Hasn't he done enough already? What of his wife and children at home in Seville? He is standing now, pushing against the table in the booth, almost shouting. All that sailing, all that vast traveling round and round, what did I think he hoped to find in the center of it? What? The whole tavern has fallen silent, waiting. He stands beside the booth, letting his shoulders slump, wondering, very quietly now, what happened to the center while he sailed the circle. Where has the center gone? The center has slipped off to the edge, perhaps, no longer inside the circle proper, and some ways beyond the point where the circle began. Is that not where he, Vespucci, belongs too? Without another word, he is gone.

I follow after him at once, but by the time I reach the sidewalk, and my eyes adjust to the afternoon glare, he is, of course, nowhere to be seen. There is nothing to do but return to my car and go on without him. Not that I will have to go it alone. Vespucci has returned to find his center, wherever it is, and doubtless I should now do the same, being careful to keep it with me, henceforth, on all my perimeters. The car, left on a side street, has been, I find, ticketed for overtime parking. I have been here too long, it's time to get moving. I won't bother to pay the parking ticket; I'm not likely to be through here again. But it was interesting meeting a man like that, wasn't it? Perhaps he wouldn't have been the ideal person for me to have traveled with: we'd have driven each other to distraction with our mutual worries before the journey was half over.

But just look at him one more time. What does history care for his personal problems? Banker, spy, opportunist—was he not, after all, the perfect man for us to have been named after? A dependable agent for the Old World's most influential commercial organization, he did what a good spy always does: he managed to be in the right place at the right time. He was there, you know, standing on the Quay at Palos—no doubt already scanning the newly opened horizons—on that spring day in 1493 when Columbus disembarked from his first voyage. He was there at Gianotto Berardo's shipfittinhouse in Seville in the years that followed to collaborate—to keep a watchful eye out—on behalf of the Medicis in the preparation of vessels for Columbus' second and third expeditions, his eye no doubt as much on the man as on the ships and ledgers. And he was also there, in Haiti, in September of 1499, as "navigator" under Alonso de Ojedo, whom he had just rejoined after southward explorations on his own, when an "unexpected" flare-up of tempers between the queen's new and powerful emissary and the would-be Viceroy of All the Indies resulted in Columbus being removed from command and returned to Spain in disgrace.

Yes, he was always *there*, standing slightly to one side, more or less unnoticed, his eye on the future. Amerigo! Amerigo! In the anonymous portrait of him which I have since seen, that hangs in the Uffizi, the rolled map of the New World rests easily in his arms, as if he had known it would be his all along. His face turns modestly to the side, but not without, first, the hint of a proud tilt. The somewhat sad expression he wears comes, it is quite clear, from the way he has turned down the corners of his mouth in the attempt to suppress a smile.

"Franz Kafka" by
Jorge Luis Borges

There is a story by Borges that neither
you nor anyone else has ever read, for it was written in the dialect of a
remote Andean Indian tribe among whom Borges lived briefly while
young, but whose language no one else knows. Borges himself seems
to have little memory of the language at this late date; with his failing
eyesight he can no longer decipher the curious symbols which he has
used to represent it on the printed page; and no one else either knows
what sounds the symbols were supposed to represent or would be
likely to pronounce them properly if he did. Meanwhile, an article in
a recent issue of the *Journal of Anthropology* has reported the finding, by an expedition from the University of Pennsylvania, of the village where Borges lived, or where, according to rough estimates
given by Borges himself after his return many decades ago, it seems
likely that he lived. No signs of recent human habitation were found
in the village, however, and the expedition has reported convincing
evidence that the population was destroyed by a sudden flare up of
venereal disease, perhaps resulting from contact with western civili-
zation, probably before World War II. Althought they left many artifacts behind, there is no evidence of their having possessed an alpha-
bet, hence no record of their language. They appear, according to
the report, to have been a marginal society of hunters and gatherers;
they kept no domestic animals; they dwelt in rather small shelters
made of unhewn stone and did their cooking over open, communal
fires; the majority of them, it appears, were left-handed; almost all of
their pottery, as well as some of the stones of the huts, is decorated
with drawings of insects, some quite crudely and some in very realis-
tic detail. Not all of the insects depicted on these objects are believed

63

to be indigenous to the region, though no suitable explanation for this phenomenon has yet been proposed.

Borges, for his part, claims not to remember what the story—which he wrote either while still residing in the village or immediately after his return—is about, but is under the impression that he included much of it in a later story, with a different setting, possibly European. A former student and present colleague of mine, Charles Morley Baxter, who interviewed Borges in Buenos Aires in 1967, tried again and again to turn the questioning in the direction of this story, only to receive instead lengthy, impassioned, and knowledgeable disquisitions on German mystics of the seventeenth century, the English prose romance, and some early twentieth-century French symbolistes of whom he had never heard before. When he asked, at last, whether it would be possible to see the "mysterious" manuscript, Borges at once reached into the drawer of a nearby desk and presented him with a sheaf of hand-written pages. These, however, turned out to be, so far as Baxter could tell, the rough draft of an unpublished essay on the palace at Knossos by the Chilean archeologist Alfonso Quenardo, whose work, though my friend was not at the time aware of this, has long since been discredited for being speculative and nonempirical.*

Nonetheless, as everyone knows by now, pirated copies of the manuscript are in common circulation among Borges aficionados throughout the world. Generally they exist in mimeographed form, though sometimes in Xerox copies (made, in all likelihood, from mimeographed versions), and, less frequently, in painstakingly handmade versions, more than one of which has already been offered me, in the several years since I began to explore this subject, as the original. Never have I seen a printed version. At this time, I have in my possession over twenty copies, in one form or another. Most of them are identical in almost all aspects: regardless of format, each fills

---

*In 1924 Quenardo rejected a sizable government grant under which he was to have headed an international archeological expedition to Crete, claiming that he could learn as much about labyrinths in Santiago as anywhere else and that "one does not have to dig in order to get dirty." These remarks, called arrogant by his colleagues and the press, severely damaged his academic career.

nine standard 8½ x 11 pages; differences, for the most part, are minor, consisting primarily of malformed symbols; there are only a few copies that reveal the addition or omission of a group of symbols, and it seems likely that these are the result of someone's attempt to compensate for a failure in the copying mechanism. It would be no great task to collate the various copies in my possession in order to produce a "good text"; such a task would be a pointless one, however, since the text has no "meaning." Cryptography could at best substitute another set of symbols—i.e., romanic letters—for the extant ones, but could bring us no closer to a successful translation; it has, to date, failed to find a consistent basis for achieving even the first task. The manuscripts rest with me still, though I have some time since given over completely the notion of seeking a "translation" and have, of late, begun to suspect Borges' use of the term *story*—if, indeed, it was he who applied that term to this work. Professor Arthur Efron, of the State University of New York at Buffalo, has persuaded me to place these documents, as well as any others collected in the interim, in the Contemporary Literature Manuscript Collection of that fine institution when my own work with them is completed, and so indeed I shall do.

In the meantime, I have been shocked to discover the proliferation of not just the manuscripts but the symbols themselves, a phenomenon I encountered in a most curious way. On my most recent visit to New York, some six months back, I spent an evening with my friend, the poet C. W. Truesdale, discussing both Borges, to whose work I had introduced him a year or so previously, and my own preoccupation with the "mysterious" manuscript, a copy of which I had with me at the time, having been given it* only that afternoon by another poet friend who had recently brought it back with him from Mexico City. While we discussed Borges, Truesdale's younger daughter, Stephanie, came in and sat down on the arm of her father's chair,

---

*I have never yet been able to *purchase* a copy; each time I have heard of the existence of one, tracked it down, and then offered to buy it, payment has been refused and it has been forced on me as a gift, in such a way as to make my refusal of it impossible.

just across from me. She had been there for some time—perhaps an hour or more, not at all a likely thing for a nine-year-old—listening intently to our conversation and playing idly with her charm bracelet, before I suddenly became aware of what I had been seeing all along: one of the charms that dangled from her bracelet was one of the symbols from the Borges manuscript! I asked at once to see the bracelet. The other charms were the ordinary ones, mementos of places visited, for the most part, which her parents had bought for her. The one with the symbol, however, was, she explained, the gift of a school friend, a shy little girl from the South who had spent a few months in Stephanie's school while her father was on an assignment in New York and then had gone away. Although Stephanie had been attracted to this child, she had never become particularly friendly with her, and so had been greatly surprised when the little girl approached her after school one day and simply handed her the charm. In spite of her knowledge of her mother's strong opposition to her accepting gifts from schoolmates, Stephanie did not for a moment consider not taking it; instead she decided to offer something valuable of her own in exchange, a beautiful polished agate that had been a gift from a friend of her parents back in Minnesota, but when she took it to school the next day she found that the girl had already been withdrawn. When she was done answering my questions in this way, Stephanie asked me why I was so interested.

"Have you ever heard of Borges?" I replied.

"Of course," she said, "you've been talking about him all evening."

The symbol that appeared on her charm was similar to the Hebrew letter *gimel*, save that the upright portion of the symbol was tilted far more to the left and the "foot" was given more of a hook, so that it looked like this:

It was the symbol that I had come to refer to, from its curious shape and the frequency of its occurrence in the manuscript, as the "grasshopper." Truesdale himself, having looked at first with some amusement upon my interrogation of his daughter, soon became quite intrigued with the matter, having at last noted that the symbol on her charm did indeed correspond with one of the symbols in the Borges manuscript which I had been showing him, and which he had been holding in his own hands for some time now. He was, all in all, interested enough to accompany me the following day on a trip to the library in an attempt to track down the sources of some of Borges' symbols in ancient or foreign alphabets, though neither of us actually expected to have much success in such a venture: Truesdale because he was not yet convinced that the whole thing was not an elaborate hoax, and myself because I could not quite believe that Borges had gotten his symbols from some "outside" source.

As it turned out, we never got to the library that day, though my later researches have demonstrated quite convincingly that the symbols—I have identified sixty-three of them quite definitively, and there are some half dozen others whose status is less certain since they may be only variations on, or malformations of, other symbols—are not derived from any other alphabets, ancient or modern. There are, to be sure, some few, such as the one noted above, in which the casual viewer might see some relations to Hebrew, or Telagu, or Arabic, but such resemblances are merely superficial, are in all cases only vague similarities and not identities, and are, in any event, not of sufficient number to warrant serious consideration.

Far more interesting, from my own point of view, was Truesdale's remark as we left for the library the following morning—he had stayed up most of the night with the copy of the manuscript that I had left behind for his examination—that he had been inspired by my own informal name for the symbol that appeared on Stephanie's charm bracelet to note that a great many of the symbols seemed to bear rough resemblances to insects. It was, I believe, the last time he ever spoke to me of this manuscript or its author. While I was still mulling over the implications of his statement, we passed a newsstand where we both observed, in the same speechless moment, that the model on the cover of the current *Harper's Bazaar* was wearing a pin in the shape of the same symbol that had appeared on the charm. It was not long before we began to see the symbol elsewhere—on the hood ornament of a foreign automobile, carved into the granite block of a cornerstone, scrawled in crayon on an advertisement for a Broadway musical comedy—and then other symbols as well—one embossed on the side of a businessman's briefcase, two appearing in an alternating pattern on the fabric of a dress in the window of a fashionable shop, another on a decal affixed to the rear window of a taxi —all within a few blocks. Truesdale's spirits began to fluctuate wildly as these things came to our attention. With a howl of excitement he would rush across a busy street, dragging me behind him through the dangerous traffic, to check the symbol emblazoned on a toy being sold by a street hawker, or haul me in pursuit of a young woman to examine the shape of her shoe buckle. In between these moments he would fall into a deep and speechless despondency, especially darkened when my own questioning of shop owners or pedestrians only served to reveal that they knew "nothing about" the symbol to which I called their attention, that it was "only a decoration," or that "someone had asked to put it there." + On the southwest corner of Eighth Avenue and 57th Street, Truesdale came to an abrupt halt and began to recite, in a loud voice rendered generally inaudible by the sounds of traffic and the rapidly gathering crowd, a poem he had apparently been composing all this while about—as best I could tell —the symbol we had been encountering most frequently. = When, however, he at last arrived at the crucial point where the symbol itself was to appear in the poem, he paused, unable to find a verbal equiv-

+Perhaps one reason for his speechlessness and our inability to discuss this event was the unspoken presence of a question neither of us wished to encounter because neither dared risk an answer: were all of these people truly innocent of the symbol to which they were connected or were they part of a silent conspiracy of its presence from which we alone were excluded?

=I still have in my possession a copy of this poem which I was sent soon after I left New York; I do not feel, however, that I have any right to reprint it inasmuch as the poet himself refuses either to submit it for publication or to read it at any of his public appearances. I fear it has been swallowed up by the same conspiracy of silence as the symbols.

alent for it, equally unable to go on without it. For one terrifying moment, it seemed as if the whole world had come to a standstill. It was with great relief that I got the two of us into a taxi.

Perhaps this crisis was only the result of what Truesdale had tried to incorporate in his poem. It is possible, of course, to include all sorts of "found objects" in poems—indeed, one might well ask what other sorts of objects there are to be included in poems—and most often without the poet being able to predict in advance quite what their effect will be upon his poems. But might it not be equally valid to assert that there are some "objects" that are capable of refusing to be incorporated into poetry? Perhaps it is the property of such objects to "act" rather than to be acted upon, so that though they may easily enter poems on their own—in all likelihood in the guise of other, less suspicious, objects—it is not possible for the poet himself to take hold of them, and place them in the poem, at his own disposition. And perhaps this, in turn, is only so because they are, so to speak, a poetry of their own—with, therefore, their own independence of action, and a certain resistance to having a chorus of words constructed "about" them. Borges himself, after all, has long since warned us that "it is hazardous to think that a coordination of words (philosophies are nothing else) can have much resemblance to the universe." So much, then, for a philosophy, a scientific system, a metaphysics, a mimetic literature. But what of a poetry?

He has at the same time asked us to see, with the symbolistes, that the world itself is a book—if not a "coordination of words," at least a forest of symbols, perhaps undecipherable. So too it may be for this untitled and unreadable—indecipherable—"story" that he has given us. It does not bear much, if any, "resemblance to the universe," save for the associations, possibly only personal, evoked by a few of its markings; it is, on the other hand, a veritable forest of symbols, through which, it begins to seem to me, now that I have begun to devote myself to it more and more fully (I fear it will be some time before I shall be ready to release my manuscript collection; my study is already impossibly cluttered with the multitude of symbol-bearing artifacts that I have accumulated in only the past few months;

what this brief essay on the subject may be only the beginning of I cannot imagine), one can walk endlessly, encountering such things as have never before been seen. *Not* a "coordination of words," but a conglomeration—who is to say that anything has been coordinated?—of things, symbols, presences; *not*, indeed, a "resemblance to the universe," but a universe itself, which cannot be "incorporated" into any other universe.

What Borges appears to have left us, then, is not a literature but a world—a strange, opaque, and stubborn world. And yet one cannot help being tempted to ask, seeing how closely it has approached our own now, whether it is possible to dwell in such a world. Some have seen it, that much is clear, and have perhaps attempted to enter it; hence the proliferation of manuscripts and pseudomanuscripts of the "story," and, lately, of the symbols. Others have tried to take hold of it more forcefully, and to bring it into their own spheres without due regard for its autonomy; hence the trauma resulting from Truesdale's attempt to include the symbol in the world of his own poem. And it is equally clear that many who come near it, or even touch upon it, without any knowledge of what they are approaching, are, by their very innocence it would seem, both protected from any dangers it might involve and included within its own sphere: hence the total naturalness and ease of Stephanie's wearing of the charm.

But at the same time, I begin to suspect that it is equally possible that "it," the Borgesan world, is not content simply to wait for others to come near, to enter into it, but instead moves anxiously forward on its own into the universe we already inhabit, even now permeating it with its own symbology. To what end? Perhaps it would be best if such a question as that simply was not raised. Not only does it suggest a teleology that may well not exist, but it implies other, and still more problematical, questions: If we knew to what end, would we want to avoid it? And if we wanted to avoid it, could we?

Already there are areas where it has impinged with dramatic effect, as if one of its symbols had somehow slipped through a tiny pinhole in a previously impervious membrane, and there, on the other side—on *our* side—had suddenly taken root and flowered. In the modern literature class I teach—*used* to teach—my students persist in saying that Gregor Samsa has turned into a grasshopper, though Kafka very plainly labels him a dung beetle. There is nothing I can do about it, or Kafka either: A symbol stronger than his has taken hold of "The Metamorphosis." Borges, in this sense, has "created" Kafka, unless it is Kafka who, by carving out in his story a small vacuum, disguised by the term *dung beetle*, into which the grasshopper symbol would naturally flow, has created Borges. + Meanwhile the poet Truesdale has abandoned New York for his cabin on Mocassin Lake in northern Minnesota. He seems well and cheerful, accomplishes an enviable amount of work, but refuses to fish or to fell timber for firewood. His wife explains that on some other fisherman's hook left in the mouth of some northern pike he lands—or, worse yet, imbedded deep inside the trunk of some ancient Norway pine—he fears to find such a symbol as would not be at all good for him to find, in such a place. Not long after takeoff on his flight west, the stewardess presented him with a large white box, containing a birthday cake. The box was very clearly marked with his name, and the stewardess was certain there had been no mistake, but it was *not* his birthday. Was it Rochester beneath him at that moment, or some other universe in which it *was* his birthday? When the plane landed he abandoned the cake in a locker without ever tasting it. Perhaps only now someone who has come to Minneapolis from terribly far away is approaching that same locker with the correct key. It is a struggle to stick to the use of these symbols, these words, and not to

+Most students, it appears, perform this metamorphosis of their own upon Kafka's story quite unconsciously, for they are genuinely surprised and confused when I point out the places in the text where Kafka uses the term *dung beetle*. More than one has insisted that "there must be some mistake in the text." However, one of my more remarkable students of recent years, the previously mentioned Charles Morley Baxter, has developed an extremely well-reasoned case for believing that Gregor is, indeed, not a dung beetle but a grasshopper, basing his argument on the fact that it is not the narrator himself who calls Gregor a dung beetle but rather the cleaning lady, who is concerned only with getting her work done and not with making nice distinctions between kinds of insects, who is probably quite ignorant of such distinctions anyway and by no means a reliable witness, *but through whose mistake* Kafka has very subtly implied, or permitted, the sense of grasshopper. I am not yet entirely convinced.

let those other symbols cover these very pages. Truesdale, meanwhile, has put the cake in a poem, or rather, in his own words, "there
was a poem in which there appeared a place for this cake, and no
other." The poem vibrates with the cake. But what will be found
when the locker is opened? Can Borges have given us a universe in
which it is possible to have one's cake and eat it too? Or where, better
yet, it is possible for one to have the cake while another "one" eats it?
Perhaps even at this moment "C. W. Truesdale" or "Jorge Luis
Borges," large and bearlike and quite hungry, is opening the locker.
I would imagine that the cake is still fresh. It is decorated with a
unique set of symbols which, like the cake, are sweet and edible. It is
not my birthday either, but what danger could there be in a little
taste?

A Brief Chronology of
Death and Night

My dog died in 1962. That was the
year before President Kennedy's assassination and the year after my
retirement. We were the same age. That is, I was the same age when I
retired as President Kennedy was when he was assassinated. In fact,
we weren't the same age at all. I was two years older. How it came
about that I was retired at such an early age, in surprisingly good men-
tal and physical health, is not at all relevant here. Suffice it to say that
my retirement came about by what is generally referred to, I believe,
as a mutual agreement. Not that I ever referred to it that way. Technically, my services were still at the beck and call of the university. More
power to them. In effect, however, I was a free man. The things they
put in a newspaper! The death of my dog left me freer still. Not that I
want to make a big to-do about my dog. The only point of my bringing
up anything about the dog to begin with was his death. A lot anybody
ever cared for poor old Shep.

He died in February. It was just as well. He was an unbearable
hulk. Hundreds of pounds of flaccid meat. He lay motionless all day in
a great hairy mound wherever he happened to tumble to the floor
after returning from his morning outing, emitting a variety of odors. It
was only with the greatest of effort, I imagine, that his cells had managed to differentiate themselves for development into eyes, claws, internal organs; no doubt it took a continuing effort of equal dimensions
to maintain those distinctions. The neighbors often phoned to com-
plain about him. They understood nothing, nothing at all. They probably believed everything they read in the papers.

I wanted to bury him myself, in the backyard, but the ground was
frozen so hard it was impossible to get a shovel through it. The only al-

ternative was to take him to the vet's and have him cremated. Unfortunately, I couldn't even get him into the car by myself. I tried pushing
and pulling and rolling, but it was all a waste of time. There was simply
too much of him. Already he had begun to acquire a new odor, not sig-
nificantly worse than any of the others. It had been several days since I
had first noticed that he no longer got up for even his morning outing. I
concluded he was dead, though he was, in essence, exhibiting no different behavior than he ever had before. Old Shep, who had been
with me for so many years. It was a Thursday. Only a few years before,
and I would have had some help to move him. Thursday was the day
my girlfriend came over. At 3:15. She was gone before supper, before
she was gone altogether. She knew enough to get out when the getting was good. That was two years before my retirement. Things were
just starting to get warm. We were the same age. That is, she was the
same age when she got out as I was when I retired. Actually, we weren't
the same age at all. She was two years older than I. But she was very
regular. Every Thursday afternoon at 3:15. After that, we could never
think of anything to do. She could have been a big help with Shep.

   In the end, I had to hire four teenage boys to do the job, all from
outside the neighborhood. The neighbors wouldn't let their sons.
Small-minded people like that. They bound his front legs together
and his rear legs together, and then slipped a wooden clothesline
pole between them to carry him by. But when they tried to lift him
up, the pole broke, so I had to go to the lumberyard and buy a stur-
dier one for them to use. They slung the pole over their shoulders
and carried him to the car. With some effort, they wrestled him into
the backseat. Then they climbed back out. They wouldn't ride with
me. With him. They followed in their own car, bringing the pole, which
stuck out through an open window. I might as well have carried the
pole in my car, since I had to keep a window open anyway. The only
place I ever took him was to the vet's, whenever I received a post-
card reminding me that it was time to bring him in for shots of one
sort or another. It was only a little way off. In the parking lot the boys
approached with the pole once more, slung him from it, and followed
me inside. I tried not to let them notice that I was aware that they
were letting old Shep's head bounce along the ground. In the waiting

room small dogs whimpered and crept around behind their masters' legs. Curs. The doctor came hurtling out from a back room, waving a syringe in one hand, though I had telephoned with the news, and he knew we weren't here for shots.

"Not here, you fool!" he shouted. He grabbed a pad of paper from the waiting room desk while I held the syringe for him. It was full of a lethal looking liquid, crystal clear and colorless. He bent over the edge of the desk, writing, his back to me. A small drop clung to the edge of the needle. The boys squirmed under the weight of the burden that hung from their young shoulders, and looked off into the distance. I found it hard to believe that they made syringes of such size. People in the waiting room bowed their heads to comfort their own pets, refusing to acknowledge me or mine. And weight, as well. Then the vet straightened and turned about, handing me the slip of paper with an address on it. I returned the syringe. We left, in a silent procession, rather like a safari, I thought, that had made the mistake of bringing in a royal pet, or the last of a species. We got him into the car again and set off once more. It was still Thursday, a very nostalgic day. We processed and recessed, recessed and processed. I paid the boys for their assistance at last and sent them on their way, letting them take the pole with them. If I took it home myself, the neighborhood kids would soon make off with it.

Old Shep lay on a low-slung metal cart for awhile, overlapping its edges on all sides, and then someone came and wheeled him away. Various parts trailed along on the floor. The attempt to maneuver him smoothly through the doorway was not altogether successful. In the end I myself was asked to leave. It was a simple repetition. Not a year had gone by yet. The same quiet tone, and a certain embarrassment, on both sides. I certainly didn't want to cause any trouble, I explained. It was much easier this way, I was told. Surely it wouldn't do any harm, I supposed, if I just stood silently in the background and observed. It was just that experience had taught them that that never worked out very well. The man who had taken Shep away wheeled the cart back in empty and parked it against the wall, just beside me. I appealed to him. The point was, to see the process through to its very end. Surely I had that much right. This was all

familiar territory. He listened, nodding at what I said. I noticed that
he had one foot propped up on the cart, and that the cart itself was
liberally covered with loose hairs. I placed one of my feet up on the
cart too, in order to establish a bit of cameraderie. Strangers are
always surprised when they find out that I'm a professor of chemistry.
I've always wondered if they would be equally surprised if they discovered that I was a professor of something else. Somehow or other,
the cameraderie failed to materialize. We both observed how I was
nervously using my foot to scrape loose hairs off the cart, so that already there was quite a scattering of them on the floor. He straightened up quite abruptly and wheeled the cart off to another corner of
the room, but I continued scraping with my foot until I had gathered
all the loose hairs on the floor into a single mound. Sort of old Shep
in miniature. Maybe this *was* the end of the process, as far as I was
concerned. The fact was, I met very few strangers. I wasn't even a
professor of chemistry anymore. Once again, I was asked to leave.

I sat outside in my car for some time, forced to keep the window
open though it was quite cold. There was no wind, but neither was
there any sun to be seen. The smoke from the chimney drifted
straight upwards, quite a bit of it. The number of hours I spend sitting
in my car was, I realized, quite disproportionate to the number of
miles I traveled in my car. There was a time, not very long ago, when
it seemed that I spent every afternoon sitting in my car. Not in very
exotic surroundings, either: the parking lot. Students and colleagues
wandered by. They had long since given up even nodding to me as
they passed. Not on Thursdays. Now I was sitting in my car on Thursday. A great stream of smoke billowed up, now thick and white, now
thin and grey. When I left at twilight it was still pouring forth, though
at last a little wind had come, to swirl the smoke about, and mix the
white with the grey.

Parking the car in the driveway at home, I looked at the speed-
ometer. Miles traveled, Thursday afternoon, 2.7. From home to the
vet's, from the vet's to the crematory, from the crematory home. Including a brief side trip to the lumberyard. Hours spent in the car,
same afternoon, approximately 3½. Well under a mile an hour. In
the vacant lot across the street glowed a strange shape I had never

seen there before. It was a good-sized tent, with a pointed roof, from the peak of which protruded a piece of chimney pipe, out of which poured a dark stream of smoke that was quickly ripped apart by the wind. The tent itself glowed from some inner light. I got out of the car and closed the door softly. It was already quite dark, and much too cold for me to stand out there very long. I hurried inside, intending to observe further from the living room window, but was pulled up short before I got that far. A thick, dark shape lay huddled up on the living room floor. Erase the 2.7 miles, I thought. Right back where I started. But what about all those hours? There were times when I wondered if I really was a professor of chemistry. I sat down in the nearest chair. It was a couch. Actually, it was a daybed, with a very clever mechanism that was probably badly in need of oiling by now. We used to have a lot of fun with that, it helped pass the time. I think this was the first time I had ever sat down on it by myself. At last I realized that the mound in the middle of the floor was only the old blanket I had covered Shep with while waiting for the boys to arrive.I walked around it and went to the window. Nothing at all was to be seen of the tent. Just then the streetlight in front of my house came on. It was 7:30, the time it always came on, winter or summer, regardless of what time the sun went down. I had often wondered on what basis such a compromise with sunset had been worked out, and by whom. In the glow I could see that the tent was still there, just as before, no longer lit from within, given to slight movements in the wind. I turned to leave the window. There was a shattering of glass. I turned back. The streetlight had been extinguished, and the tent was no longer visible.

It was very much in evidence the following morning, for what I had not been able to see in the fading twilight or the faint glow of the streetlight was that it was painted in gaudy stripes of purple and gold, like the tent of a sheik on a real desert. A small beast, tied to one of the front tent stakes, yelped and jumped about, a miniature poodle if I wasn't mistaken, though I have had little contact with dogs of pedigree. As I stood watching, still in my pajamas, a cup of coffee in my hand, a police car pulled up in front of my house. For some time it just sat there. Now and then the officer in the passenger's seat glanced up towards the window where I was standing. I took a couple of steps back into the unlighted room. At last the officer who was driving got out, crossed the street, and walked up to the tent. I could still see them well enough. The poodle ignored him. The officer seemed momentarily at a loss, perhaps because there was neither doorbell to ring nor solid door to knock upon. Soon enough, however, he parted the flaps and stepped through, perhaps summoned from within. Not long after, he emerged, and returned to his car. For some time yet, the car simply sat there. Finally it pulled away.

I went off to the kitchen then for a fresh cup of coffee. The doorbell rang. It was my next-door neighbor, who hadn't so much as nodded to me in passing for well over a year now. Not that I walked about in the neighborhood a great deal. I could tell you what paper *she* read. She was well bundled up against the cold and carried a sheaf of papers in her gloved hands. Unfortunately, I was still in my pajamas. She apologized. I apologized. She could come back later. It would just take me a moment. If I didn't mind, then, it being something of an emergency.If she would just make herself comfortable. She was rather an attractive woman, somewhere around my own age. It was her children I despised. But they were grown and out of the house now, and, so far as I could tell, no longer much in evidence. Other neighbors had informed me that her husband, who was already no longer in evidence many years ago when I first entered the neighborhood, was a man many years her senior who, shortly after fathering those several children, had run off and joined the navy of some foreign country. By the time I returned dressed, she had taken off her coat and seated herself on the edge of the couch.

"I suppose you know why I'm here," she said.

"The police have already been around," I informed her.

"It's no use," she said. I went over and looked out the window. A thin trail of smoke was coming from the chimney pipe. She explained that she had already checked it out quite thoroughly. For a small sum the man who had pitched the tent there had purchased a long-term option to buy the land which included a clause granting him the privilege of making whatever use he wanted of the land during the term of the option, so long as the use was legal and no permanent structures were erected on the land. The block, on which this was the only vacant lot, was, of course, zoned for single-family residences, requiring building permits before any structure was begun, but the county attorney had expressed some doubts as to whether a tent would qualify as a "structure" under the building code. Moreover, he had informed her, there was a law dating back to the homesteading days of the last century which gave any landholder the right to erect a temporary shelter on his property while deciding what further use to make of it; such rights would no doubt accrue to the holder of an option as well.

"But it can't be for too long," I protested. "Undoubtedly the option will expire soon."

"On the contrary," she explained, "it's both renewable and transferable."

"Is it really so bad?" I objected. It was her own sons, as I remembered, who had always pitched tents there in the past. "Most of the year it's only a mass of weeds anyway, as well as a common dumping ground."

"But," she cried, waving her armload of papers wildly about, "there's a *man* in there!" On the downswing, her arm brushed the edge of the couch and activated its unique internal mechanism, long unused. Without the slightest creak it swung gracefully open into a daybed. It didn't need oiling after all. She went sprawling across it, papers flying. "My petitions!" she cried.

"What kind of man is he?" I asked. I suppose I should have offered to help her up. She lay on her back, her skirt twisted up around her hips, her feet dangling off the edge, almost touching the floor.

"As if you didn't know!" she said. I was still standing over by the window, looking out at the tent. But what could possibly have happened to bring forth an exclamation like that? And yet she didn't move. Perhaps there was something I ought to do. I hurried across the room toward her and began to gather up the scattered petitions from around the daybed where she still sprawled. She had quite nice legs. I offered to sign one of her petitions. For a long time she said nothing at all. I stacked the petitions into a neat pile. Truly fine legs.

I laid the pile on the daybed beside her. She looked very peaceful there.

"Would you really do that?" she said, at last. She raised herself up on her elbows and stared me straight in the eye.

"Why not?" I asked. "After all, I live here too." I unclipped one of the pens in my shirt pocket.

"Look," she said. Before I could sign the petition, she got up from the daybed, straightened her skirt, brushed her hand lightly over her hair, and beckoned me to follow her across to the window. Led me across, when I paused to put my pen away. She actually took me by the arm. And there he was, when we got there, standing right out in front of his tent.

"Look at him! " she said. I did. He was standing there very casually, poorly dressed for the weather I thought, holding his dog loosely on the leash, surveying the neighborhood about him. As if it were his. The dog leapt up and down at the end of the leash.

"Don't you see! " she said. I did. He was thin and bespectacled, with a small moustache and greying hair.

"I never saw him before in my life," I told her.

"But he looks just like you! "

"I wouldn't say that," I said. That's not a very convincing denial, she told me. You're merely going on superficial resemblances, I charged, what do you know of the real me, or even the real him? Enough, she said. For example? I asked. He's a graduate student, she said, in comparative literature. A young fool, I suggested. Not at all, she said, you've seen his grey hair yourself. And still working on his doctorate, I chortled, all those years, why I had mine when I was twenty-six, by the time I was thirty. . . . In the humanities, she snapped, it takes longer. Besides, she said, he didn't start till he was older than you. Not older than you were when you started, but older than you are now. Ha, by the time he's finished, he'll be dead. That's soon enough. Soon enough for what? Just soon enough.

It seemed an interminable bit of bickering. I hardly knew the woman. Not a word of consolation from her about old Shep, either. Just a lot of hysteria. Accusations and innuendoes. While the subject of it all was no longer to be seen. Back inside his tent, probably, working on some grimy little piece of pseudoscholarship. I left the window and went over to put the daybed back into its proper position. There was some *real* work to be done, if only one could get past the little minds. The newspapers misrepresented it all. All.

"You lost your dog," she said. It was a simple statement of fact. I turned about from examining the daybed, trying to remember what it was one did, to set it right. She was silhouetted in the window, quite a lovely figure.

"Yesterday," I said. Could she have helped me cart him off to the crematorium? Slight as she was, she looked like she had a certain strength about her.

"*He's* got a dog," she said. Forcefulness, rather. As if I hadn't seen it for myself already. A jumpy, nervous little thing, that probably never did settle down. What could you do with a beast like that? That had nothing whatsoever to do with old Shep. I turned back to the daybed. It could hardly be a very complicated mechanism, if it was meant to be used in the ordinary household. It had just been a long time since I had used it.

"I'm sorry," she said. She had crossed over toward me from the window. It was a very generous thing for her to say. Even though she had probably never even petted him, in all these years. I straightened up to thank her.

"About the couch," she said. Daybed, I snapped. I seem to have caused you a bit of trouble, she apologized. I informed her that it was nothing serious. Does it do that often? she asked. I told her I hadn't even been aware that it was working. Oh yes, she giggled, it works just fine. Now if I could only get it back the way it belongs. She offered to help. Do you use if often? she asked. We stood at opposite ends. Truthfully, I said, no. I instructed her to lift up on the front corner. Whatever happened to the young woman who used to visit you? she asked. We both lifted on the corners. Not so young, I told her. Something groaned from within. But very regular, she said. She smiled at me. We pushed in on it a bit, gently. She went away, I said. It folded inward and the back of the couch thrust itself up. There it is, I said.

The Discovery of America

That wasn't so difficult after all, she said. We smiled at each other, and then sat down upon it to test it out. It was a pleasure to see things resuming their normal shape once more. Her hands were folded in her lap. She looked very comfortable sitting there. But I supposed that it was time for me to sign her petition and let her go on her way. Now, I started to say. Suddenly the back of the couch flipped back down, the front shot straight forward, and the whole thing extended itself into its daybed position once more, throwing us both wildly about as it did so, so that we ended up twisted curiously together, her mouth buried in my neck, mine in her hair, her arms around me, my hands. . . . my hands. She wore no stockings and the skin on the inside of her thigh was unbelievably soft. No, she was soft all over, in the way her mouth moved, first on my neck and then on my own mouth, in the way her arms moved around me and her body molded itself softly against mine, in the way her thighs first pressed warmly together on my hand and then moved apart as my hand moved along them and then opened fully into the dampness of her crotch and then edged about, just so, to help me slide her pants down, and in the way she flowed about me, *all* about me, as I unzipped my fly and fumbled my swollen cock out and edged it easily into her, in the same liquid way she slid her tongue far back into my mouth, and we both began to move together, ever so softly, until a great gentle wave came rolling over us, through us, and the daybed beneath us at last gave forth one small creak. There was something we had done wrong, I realized, in trying to set it up as a couch, that it didn't stay that way. But I was much too soft myself, just now, to get a firm grip on what the problem was. It was altogether too easy just to let myself be moved about, as she slid gently out from underneath me, and edged me over slightly, and began to remove my clothing, item by item, and to toss each item onto a pile in the center of the floor, and then slid her dress and slip up over her head, and threw them onto the pile, and unhooked her bra, and tossed it after. There were two shpaeless piles in the center of the floor. One, our clothing, and the other, old Shep's blanket, still there. She lay back and reached over toward me. It hadn't even been twenty-four hours. Her breasts were large but soft and nearly shapeless, and the nipples rose to meet my touch just as I felt my cock rising to meet the touch of her hand that came to draw me into her once again. I moved between the legs she opened for me. Her breast moved softly beneath my fingers. Her mouth moved open around my mouth as I moved down over her. Old Shep wouldn't have moved even if he had been there. We both moved together. And still alive. The daybed moved beneath us, whispering against our skin. Flesh moved. Moved. It was a motion, I thought, that could go on forever. Wrong again. We moved together up an enormous slope. Nothing goes on forever. And tumbled over its summit. But you do want to see things through to the end. Then we lay motionless.

But then we began again with the hands, moving them over each other. Nothing ever quite ends, either. Those soft, fluid breasts, nipples sunken back into them. Thighskin and scrotum. A hair in the corner of her mouth. Dark, shapeless stain between us on the daybed when at last we sat up. It never stops, she said. What's that? I asked. She said, The thing is, to get it going. I cupped a breast in the palm of my hand. But what does it take? she said. I didn't know then. I bent to kiss the breast I held, and felt the nipple harden between my lips. He said, That's the great mystery, she said. I lifted my head. He said? I said. How long it takes, she said. Who he? I said. Our new neighbor, she said. I let go of her breast. Then you've talked with him, I said. Yes, she said. She took my hand and put it back on her breast. You seem to know a lot about him, I said. Yes, she said. She pulled my other arm around her, to hold her other breast. But, I said, he's only been here since yesterday. She said, I spent the night with him. The night? I said. She held my hands to her breasts. If you had another hand, she said, I'd put it between my legs. And then you came over here to me? I said. Yes, she said, you really do look just like him. Hardly, I said. But you saw, she said. From a distance, I said. Then come and see, she said. She got up and sorted out our clothes. Why? I said. So you can see for yourself, she said. She tossed me my clothes. No, I said, why did you come over here? Perhaps he sent me, she said, pulling her slip down over her head. With petitions? I said. He's collected them from other places, she said, it was a way to get in. To make love with me? I said. To bring you over there, she said. Why? I said. Zip me, she said, and tuck your shirt in, in back. As we were putting our coats on, she noticed the pile that remained in the center of the floor.

"What's that?" she asked.

"Old Shep's blanket," I told her.

"The dead dog," she said.

"Yes," I said.

"What did you do with him?" she asked.

"Had him cremated," I told her.

"That was the easiest way," she said. We were already at the door. I looked back at the empty blanket huddled there in the center of the floor. I supposed I'd have to dispose of it now.

"Frankly," I said, "it was a mess." I opened the door.

"What will you do with the ashes?" she asked. I pushed the little button to leave the door unlocked and pulled it shut behind us. Outside, the wind was howling wildly.

"What ashes?" I asked. But apparently she didn't hear me. Did they give you your dog's ashes? She took my hand and led me quickly across toward the tent. Was I supposed to wait for them yesterday, or had I ought to go back for them today? The wind whipped right along behind us. Did they give you an urn, too, or did you have to provide your own? There wasn't a wisp of smoke coming from the chimney pipe that poked out of the top of the tent. What would I do with the ashes, anyway? Store them away? Set them out on display? Scatter them? Scatter them.

The tent was empty. When she lifted the flap, all was dark inside. Neither the man nor his dog was anywhere to be seen. We stepped inside together and let the flap fall back into place behind us. Our eyes slowly grew accustomed to the gloom. The only sound was the flapping of the canvas in the wind. In the center was a little potbellied stove, from which a pipe rose through the top of the tent. It still gave off heat, though there no longer seemed to be any fire burning in it. In one corner, a mattress, piled high with neatly folded blankets. At its side, a brightly polished kerosene lamp, a gas can, a large box of wooden matches. Along the opposite wall, a card table, its top badly scratched and faded, laid out flat on the floor, its legs folded beneath it. Next to it, a small metal trunk. Not much, altogether. No dog, no urn, no ashes. It was quite warm. The fact was, the stove was packed with ashes. Between the hole in the roof that accommodated the stovepipe and the front flap that whipped about in the wind, quite a lot of light came in. Enough to see the gaudy stripes of the outside repeated on the inside as well. And the bucket of coal behind the stove. And a small stool just inside the doorway behind us, on which to place our folded coats, for it was much too warm to stand around in them any longer. Then she took my hand and used it as a pointer to go around the room once more, though I had already seen everything there. "Plenty of blankets," she said, starting on the right. "Kerosene lamp makes a lovely, gentle light. Takes very little to keep it warm in here." Our hands were actually sweating. "Table legs aren't sturdy enough to hold it up, but the surface is usable. Trunk is full of books." It was. That was a long time ago. They were in no order whatsoever. Just as if they had been tossed in there in a great hurry. Or as if someone had been rummaging about in there for some particular book he was in great need of. Either way, you could see how important it was for him, either that he got all those books in there or that he got out the one that he wanted. The dim light and the warmth were making me quite drowsy. What I really wanted, was to lie down on that mattress for just a bit, and pull a couple of those blankets over me. It was surprising how cozy it was, for such a cold windy day. How warm her hands were. I pulled her very close to me. Just then the flap blew open in the wind, and in the bright moment before it fell back into place, I saw that there was someone standing in my doorway across the street. I was equally surprised to see how late it was already. Hadn't it still been morning when we came over to the tent? What's more, the front door was wide open. "Now who could that be?" I said. Together we edged the flap open. Just a conspiratorial slit. The afternoon light was rapidly fading.

"Look at him!" she said. It was clear enough, who it was over there. Looking just like a . . . a professor of something or other. It was the year before the year before. He was on his way out to deliver a lecture that would open some eyes here and there. Early evening. Did it really happen like that? Perhaps he was just returning from the lecture, quite satisfied with the way things had gone. Hardly any light left. Things went on and on. What if the fools didn't understand. Things went on, all the same, that was how they went. Further and further. He held a leash in his hand, but the dog at the other end was already in the house, out of sight. The thing was, to see them through. Soon it would be night. He looked around over the neighborhood, using his other hand to hold the collar of his overcoat tightly closed. Right to the very end. The mystery was that it happened so quickly and yet took so much time. It was dark already. We let the tent flap drop.

The Real Meaning of the Faust Legend

Who is there who isn't peddling himself to the devil in some way? There are those who do it according to the tradition: for knowledge and power. There are those who do it for fame and money. There are those who do it to maintain the status quo and those who do it for the sake of revolution. There are those who do it to keep their children fed, to quiet their own consciences, to make the sun rise tomorrow morning, or to torment their heirs. There are those who do it for what most of us might agree are sufficiently good reasons, and others whose reasons, well, leave something to be desired. Why do I do it? I do it for a .368 batting average.

Fame, you might say. Not hardly. I don't hit that for the Reds or the White Sox. Not even for Indianapolis or Louisville. I hit it for Muncie of the Three-I League. I never wanted the fame, believe me; I only wanted to hit .368. And not even that on a regular basis. I wanted it as a lifetime average. The nice thing about that is that it leaves a lot to chance: I might hit .318 one season, but I might also hit .427—as, in fact, I did three years ago. The logical question, of course, is how fame can fail to come to one who hits consistently up there where I do, but the answer is equally logical. I hit it for Muncie. In other words, I have had many chances higher up—have them most every spring, as a matter of fact. Muncie is a farm club, after all. So there I am down in Tampa or Sarasota every March, and people who know what I did at Muncie last year are watching me each time I take batting practice, and all those out-of-shape big league pitchers who are sweating off their bellies doing laps around the outfield are just waiting for the first intersquad game. And with good reasons, too, because they know how good I'm going to make them look. I play on "B" teams in the Grapefruit League and end up hitting .187, so naturally when we break camp for the exhibition swing heading north, you know where I'm going.

Every year, of course, my season gets interrupted at Muncie when somebody at Denver breaks a leg or goes into a two-month-long slump and the big brass decide to call up the leading hitter in the minors to fill the gap, but for the most part my stays in the lofty altitudes of Triple A ball are mercifully short. I'm in a slump the day I suit up. I may have hit safely in the last thirty-two games for Muncie, with two or more hits in twenty of them, as is frequently the case, but suddenly I'm O for 18 before I trickle one between first and second that rolls dead before the right fielder gets to it. Once I even got peddled to the Yankees in a stretch drive, but you don't want to hear about that one. Muncie is where I always end up.

And why not? There are people who think I must be on the verge of suicide, being able to hit the way I do at Muncie and then not making it at all anywhere farther up the ladder, and my previous manager, who never hit more than .250 himself, was one of those who had the notion that all I needed to make it in the majors was confidence. But he was dead wrong. I *knew* I could hit .368, I had perfect confidence in my ability to do so; after all, I did it—or something close to it—every year, and how many ballplayers can say that, even in the minors? So Billy cost the parent club a good bit in psychologist and hypnotist bills with his silly theory, and then one summer cost himself a sizable measure of pain over his investment in double-up bets when I had a fat hitting streak in the beginning of August. I had gone 5 for 8 in a Sunday doubleheader, including a pair of bases loaded doubles in the second game, and had hit safely the last three times at bat, and on the bus home from Peoria, Billy got on my back again about the confidence thing.

"No, Billy," I told him, "you're wrong, dead wrong. I've got so much confidence I'm willing to bet you I hit .385 for the season. I'll pay you a hundred dollars for each point I hit below that and you pay me a hundred for each point above." He looked at me then and fell silent and took off his cap and scratched his head. He was obviously tempted—maybe only to see if I really had the confidence to shake hands on a bet like that—but the fact was that I was already hitting .379 and was on a pretty hot streak, so he thought better of it and shook his head no. And that was a good thing for him because I ended the season at .397. But I didn't want to let him off that easy.

"All right then, Billy," I said, because I wanted to show him just how wrong he was about his confidence theory, "how about a five-dollar bet that I get a hit first time up next game?"

Well, that was all right with him, especially since the next game, though at home, was against Des Moines, which was currently leading the league by a good twelve games and had a couple of hot young pitchers who were sure to be called up by the end of the month. That may have made a difference to Billy, but not to me. After Johnson and Feathers went down on called strikes in the first, I patted Billy on the shoulder and went up there and lined the first pitch over the third baseman's head and down into the corner for a stand-up double.

Sitting on the bench during the next inning, I asked Billy if he wanted to double up his bet on my next at bat, giving him a chance to come out five ahead. He was paying more attention to the kid on the mound than to me, but he mumbled "OK, why not?"

I didn't get a turn at the plate again till the last of the fourth with one out, because that kid hadn't allowed one out of the infield since my first inning double, and maybe Billy wasn't even thinking about our bet by then because we were losing 4–0 and he had to get a scouting report in on the kid by noon the next day. This time I waited out a couple of pitches, till I was sure Billy was watching, and then lined one up the middle. Took off my cap and waved at Billy from first base, and he just stood on the dugout steps and shook his head at me, and that was where we both stayed while the next two guys fouled out to the catcher.

When I came up again in the last of the sixth, with two out and none on, we were seven runs behind, and besides me nobody had gotten to base except the catcher, Wiltz, who had walked the inning before. Billy was juggling relief pitchers and looking very sad, so I had to shake him a bit to get his attention. He looked irritated when he turned around; as far as he was concerned it wasn't anything but a hot, lost, miserable afternoon, and there wasn't much anyone could do about it at this point. What's more, it was dragging on endlessly, for in spite of the way we were being set down, Des Moines had kept up enough action on the bases and in our bullpen so that the game was almost two hours old already. I just stayed calm though.

"Double up again, Billy?" I asked him.

"What's that?" he said, like he didn't even know what the name of the game was.

"It was five on my first at bat," I reminded him, "and ten on my second. Want to go for twenty this time?"

"Shit," he said, squinting up at me, "that's five straight since Sunday, you can't keep that up against a kid like this. He's major league stuff."

"We're on then?"

"Right," he said as I headed for the on-deck circle, "we're on."

I was first-ball hitting again and went with the pitch, which was a nice outside slider that I lined to right just beyond the first baseman's reach. And stayed on first base again while Kryzinski struck out for the third straight time.

By the time I came up to lead off the last of the ninth, Johnson had got us a run, and our only hit besides my three, with an inside-the-park homer that the Des Moines outfielders, worn out from chugging around the bases all afternoon, just didn't seem to have the energy to run down. Billy, who had just finished calling me a smart-assed old man but had agreed all the same to one more bet, for forty dollars this time, was standing by the water cooler shaking his head. And the kid on the mound, who could understand the stupidity that had led to the home run but couldn't understand how I had hit him three straight times, was grinding the ball in his glove and glaring at me. I was thirty-five bucks ahead and would be out only five even if I lost this time, and besides I wasn't arrogant enough to really think I could go on getting consecutive hits forever, so I decided I would at least have a little fun. He was throwing hard but sharp and obviously wanted to get me this time, as I'm sure he had a right to. He wanted to be a major leaguer, that was what he was peddling himself to his devil for. His first two were curve balls strikes and I just let them go by with no intention of swinging. I was ready on the next, but it was low and away. Then he came in with the fast ball, and 1 and 2, nine to one, forty dollars and all, I just let my bat hang out there in front of it and dropped a lovely little bunt down the third base line and skipped on down to first while the pitcher, catcher, third baseman, and poor Billy most of all just stood there and watched it roll dead on the grass as if they'd never seen such an obscene thing in the middle of a ball field before.

Now I wasn't at all worried about that kid pitcher, even if he did blow sky-high after my bunt and walk the next two men on eight straight pitches. He was going to be a major league star and that was all there was to it. Fame, money, and women, and nothing short of a broken back in an automobile accident or an all-out war was likely to stop him. I even doubted if war could. He'd probably turn up 4-F in the spring and pitch 300 innings that same season. So naturally with the bases loaded and no one out in the last of the ninth, he struck out Henry on a 3 and 2 count and got Goldburg to bounce into a double play. That kid was no different from anybody else, just a particularly obvious case.

I was more worried about Billy, who was already muttering, even as we walked off the field, about getting it back tomorrow afternoon. He was also an obvious case, in a way. I think he never really wanted to be a hitter, even though he broke in on a long ball reputation, but mostly just wanted to be in baseball, somehow or other. So when he found out what it was like, standing up there at the plate four, five times a game, he bargained himself into a managership. Now he didn't know that was going to mean seven years at Muncie, but you deal for a managership and you get a managership; nothing guarantees it's going to be in Detroit or San Francisco. If he'd peddled himself for Detroit he could have surely have had that, but maybe he'd have ended up there as a used-car salesman, who knows. Also he didn't know that every time he put a decent team together he'd be

raided in the middle of the summer by the parent club and end up finishing the season with the same rag-tag bunch that had come in 24½
games behind the year before. He didn't know he'd have to live with
things like his big dumb catcher slipping on the dug-out steps and
stomping down on the toe of tomorrow's starting pitcher in the
middle of today's dismal loss. Yes, and there was that poor kid, who
hadn't yet made up his mind whether or not this was what he wanted
to peddle himself for, sitting in the locker room watching his big toe
swell up bigger and bigger. It was time for him to decide. And poor
Billy surely didn't know he'd end up the day $75 in the hole, with
$80 riding on the first inning of the next day's game, to a thirty-five-
year-old left fielder who was an eleven-year veteran of a minor
league team he not only couldn't hit his way off of, even with the
leading average in the Three-I League for eight of those years—to
say nothing of the longest stay on record at Muncie—but didn't even
seem to care about.

"Al," he said, when we were having a beer at McDougal's after
the game, "when are you going to grow up and do something with
your life?"

"Billy," I told him, "I am doing something with my life. I'm hitting .386 after today's game." He looked up at me and emptied the
pitcher that was on the table between us into his own mug. He hadn't
paid up yet, but I supposed that as long as I was ahead, even if only
on the books, I was going to have to buy the beers, so I carried the
pitcher over to the bar for a refill. When I came back he was waiting
with an empty glass.

"Look," he said, while I filled it for him, and then poured myself
one as well, "why don't you be a good boy and go hit .386 for the
Pirates, or the Yokahama Giants, if that's what'll make you happy?"

"Billy," I told him, "I am happy." But he went right on as if he
hadn't even heard me.

"Maybe you'll have to settle for .322, or even an occasional
season at .298, but you could do it, Al, I know you could. All you
need's a little confidence."

"Billy," I reminded him, "I've got plenty of confidence. Didn't I
already show you that today?"

"You smart-assed college kids are all alike," he muttered, finishing the pitcher off again. "You get a little lucky and right off you think you know it all." He pushed the empty pitcher across at me.

"Billy," I reminded him when I came back, "I'm not one of your smart-assed college kids that comes and goes here. I may have gone to college, but that was a long time ago, when I didn't know what I wanted yet, and you don't see me tripping on my degrees while I'm running the bases, do you? I'm no kid, either, Billy, I'm as old as you, or maybe a little bit older. And I didn't get lucky, as you damn well know, unless you want to say I've been lucky for the past eleven years. No, Billy, what I had was confidence that I could go up and get a hit each one of those times today, and I've got confidence I can do it first time up tomorrow, too, if you're still on, and for as long after that as you want to keep it up." I got up to leave, before I got stuck buying another pitcher.

"On," he said. Feathers and Goldburg were standing at the table by then, and when they heard that the bet was still on for tomorrow, they wanted a piece of the action too. But this was strictly between Billy and me, so when I left, the two of them were sitting on either side of Billy trying to arrange a bet between just themselves. Billy, between them, had his chin in his hands and was staring at the empty beer pitcher.

I had three hits in the first four innings the next day, including a single, a double, a triple, and five rbi's before Billy pulled me out with the excuse that we were already eight runs ahead and put old Falucci in for me. Falucci had always wanted to have the strongest arm in baseball, and he probably did. He could throw strikes across the plate from anywhere in the outfield. But he couldn't hit well enough to stick on any team, and so he had spent a couple of decades bouncing around from one minor league club to the next and never getting in enough playing time to fulfill his dream of throwing out all those runners at the plate. Meanwhile, it had become a real obsession with him: everything hit to him he fired to the plate, whether it was a bases empty single or a fly ball with a man on first. You had to have a sharp catcher, which we didn't, to remember to be ready for a Falucci peg every time somebody banged one to left. But meanwhile, we were ahead 13 – 5 when I went out, I was glad to see the lefty with the swollen toe was determined to hang in there long enough to pick up the win, and I now had ten straight hits and $635 of Billy's money, though I had yet to see any of his real cash.

Thursday, when I came in from left field after the top of the first, I saw that someone had propped a chalkboard up on the bench in the dugout and was keeping a record of the progress of our running bet. It read "11—$640" and then further over on the same line it said "$1275," which was the total of what Billy would owe me if I got a hit the first time up. I did. Johnson walked leading off, Feathers drilled one to right on the hit-and-run, and I bounced one off the left field wall, scoring both of them.

When I came up again in the third, we were ahead 3 –0 on Wiltz's second inning triple and a wild pitch, and the chalkboard read "12—1280—2555." I looked over at Billy from the on-deck circle and he looked grim but he shook his head up and down. They didn't give me much to hit at this time, but I was determined not to take a walk, even though that wouldn't have lost the bet for me but only postponed it till my next at bat. I got the first two pitches in the dirt and the next one behind my back. The 3 and 0 pitch was a curve spinning low and away, but I went for it all the same, got underneath it just like I wanted, and lofted it high down the right field line. It stayed up there, in the still air under dark clouds that were building up all around us, and dropped over the fence just inches inside the foul pole.

By the last of the fifth, Des Moines had gone ahead 6– 4, the chalkboard read "13—2560—5115," and when I stepped up to the plate with two outs and McKay, who had singled for the pitcher, on first, the thunderstorm that had been threatening suddenly broke and sent us all scampering for the dugouts. We sat for forty-five minutes and watched the heavy downpour before the umpires called it off and Billy, who had been deep in silent thought all the while, carefully pointed out to me that since the game had now been canceled and wouldn't appear in the record books, my two hits were wiped out, and so were his losses for the day. I couldn't argue with him and didn't want to.

Friday it rained all day so Des Moines went home, and Saturday, when Ft. Wayne came to town, the field was still too soggy to play on, so Saturday's game was rescheduled as part of a Sunday doubleheader. But when Billy fell suddenly quiet after standing there in the locker room Saturday afternoon telling us that, I could see just what was going through his head. Even wiping out my two hits in Thursday's rained-out game, I had ten straight and he was $635 behind. A doubleheader, if I played both games—and he didn't have another left fielder except Falucci, whom he couldn't really justify using in my place unless we were way ahead—could mean as many as ten more times at bat for me for the day. He had already had a taste Thursday of what just a couple more hits could cost him, and even if I had to hit a couple more in place of those two that had been wiped out, he was clearly beginning to have his doubts. If I went to the plate four times in the first game, he'd be betting $5,120 against that fourth hit. Ten times and the bet would be up to $327,680! Which was a good bit more than he could afford. He just stood there and looked at me where I sat on the bench in front of my locker. Everybody else was picking up to leave. I just sat and stared at the floor, not wanting to look him in the eye. I didn't know whether to pick up and go myself and let him sweat it out or to take pity on him and offer to call it off, and I was afraid I'd offend him either way, which never was my aim. All I ever wanted to do was hit .368. Not even .370. I thought that zero at the end made it sound a little too astronomical, a little arrogant. Just a nice ragged .368. It didn't make any difference to me where I hit it. None at all. The fact that there were rarely more than five hundred fans in the stands or that I wasn't getting $100,000 a season or that I didn't have my picture on trading cards, my signature on bats, and Marilyn Monroe on my arm didn't bother me in the least. It wasn't fame or fortune I peddled myself for. It was, as I said, a .368 average.

When I looked up, Billy was gone and so was everyone else. The locker room was empty, and damp and chilly from two days of rain, and I felt pretty much the same way myself. I went home and tried to watch the nationally televised game, Senators at Boston, but both teams seemed to be trying to set a major league record for pop-ups, and I couldn't stand that sort of boredom for long. Watching someone else play was never my idea of baseball anyway. I strolled down to McDougal's but when I looked in the window and saw Billy sitting at a table with half a dozen of my teammates around him, I felt too embarrassed to go in and join them. Instead I went back home and with some trouble got my old Ford started—I never used it much during the season because you can't hop around all day and night if you want to hit .368, that's part of the price—and went and had dinner by myself at the Country Kitchen and then came back in to the Drive-In and sat and ate popcorn and watched a horror movie triple-feature until 1:30 A.M.

Sunday was bright and clear again and not too hot. We even had a decent crowd, for a change. And Billy had a surprise for me. Ft. Wayne scored twice in the top of the first, mostly on walks and a couple of errors. When I came in from left field Billy was standing on the dugout steps holding my bat out to me.

"Don't sit down," he said, "You're leading off."

"Billy?" I said. What was he trying to do, pushing it like that? Why, leading off I might even get a couple more at bats in, as he had to know. The chalkboard was still there in the dugout, but it was lying under the bench and there was nothing written on it, as if whoever had thought it up in the first place had realized it was a bad joke and was now trying to ignore it. A little calculating on the way to the plate told me that a pair of extra chances, beyond the ten I'd already figured on for the afternoon, would get our bet up over a million dollars. I didn't know whether to laugh or cry.

But one way or another, I didn't wait. Their first game pitcher was an aging major leaguer sent down to work out some midseason shoulder miseries, but from what I could see of his warm-up pitches he hadn't worked out much of anything yet. I stepped up, tugged at my cap, tried to smile over at Billy but couldn't spot him right off in the dugout shadows, and cocked my bat. The first pitch was right down the pipe and had nothing on it. I took my swing and sent it bouncing on nice even hops right out to the shortstop. Then, just to make sure, in case that damn fool high school kid let it go through his legs without touching it, I fell down on my way to first base.

Billy didn't have a great deal to say to me for the rest of the season after that. He let me stay in the number one slot, which was all the same to me, and I finished the year, like I said, at .397. When we had our final little get-together at McDougal's after the last game and just before everybody took off, most of them to play winter ball in Mexico or the Caribbean, Billy to go back to his wife and kids in New Jersey, he seemed a little sad and distant, and not much interested in all the beer that was flowing. We hadn't been there more than an hour before he stood up and announced he had to get on his way. He said goodbye and thanked everybody and then went around the tables, shaking hands with each of us. I was last. When he came to me, I got up and walked to the door with him. At the door I shook his hand and then reached into my pocket and took out a five-dollar bill, which was what I still owed him from all those bets, and tried to give it to him, but he wouldn't take it

"Use it to buy the boys some more beer with," he said, and then he turned and left. I did, and then I left too.

Next season we had a new manager, a redheaded wild man, and I heard that Billy was managing Amarillo in the Texas League. Red, who had been a fine catcher till arthritis had started creeping into all his broken finger bones and knuckles, had the idea that a manager's job was to manage as much as possible, so he juggled the outfield around every couple of days or so and had me batting everywhere in the lineup but ninth. I never knew from one day to the next what field I'd be playing or where I'd be hitting. Curiously enough, we weren't doing any worse than under Billy. But it was all very unsettling for me, and the result was that around midseason I found myself in the midst of the worst year I could remember. I was hitting .306, watching a lot of fat ones go by, and settling for a hit a game, mostly singles at that. Red wasn't very happy with either my attitude or my style of play and was platooning me with a fat farm boy who had a penchant for hitting tremendous homers with the bases empty and then striking out four times in a row with men on. But what did all that have to do with what I really wanted to do? Nothing, I realized, and then took off.

It was a Fourth of July doubleheader, and when I went four for five in the first game Red let me stay in for the second. I picked up three more hits in that one and kept on going. I had the hottest three weeks anybody ever saw. By the end of July, even with that chubby strikeout king getting his chances now and then, I was over .350 and going strong, even though Red still couldn't decide whether to have me bat first, third, or fifth. We were in Peoria and had just won the last of a three-game sweep with a 9–0 shutout in which I'd walked twice and then banged out three straight doubles to the exact same spot in left center. When I came out of the shower, I found Red waiting for me next to my locker. He sat on the bench and smoked a cigar without saying a word while I dressed, then he asked me to come with him. He had driven his own car up so that he could cut over to Chicago on our off day to visit his family, so we sat in the car in the parking lot outside the ball field until he finished his cigar and threw it out the window. Then he turned to me and started telling me what a fine job I was doing for the club, and what a great hitter I was.

"I know," I told him, "I've been hitting like that for a good many years now."

"Al," he said then, "I talked to the general manager this morning." I knew just what was coming next: "He said they could use a boost in their batting order up there."

"Red," I told him, "forget it. I've been there before. I hit here." He had a sudden pleading look in his eyes. They must have offered him a fat bonus if he could send someone up who would have a hot bat for the next few weeks. Even an old man like me.

"Look, Al," he said, "you can do it, I know you can. I've watched you hit. All you need is a little confidence." That did it.

"Red," I asked him, "what am I hitting?" He told me without even having to look it up: .357, including today's game.

"Red," I said, "that's not what I mean. I want to know what's my lifetime average." That took him back a bit, but since he was a hot one for managing and a demon for statistics, he was carrying all the club's record books with him. He reached over and got the big cumulative team book out of the backseat, along with the current season's book and a pencil and pad of paper. Then he lit up another cigar and sat and figured and chewed on it and relit it a couple of times and finally turned back in my direction.

"Well," he said, "I've checked it and double checked it and it keeps coming out the same. Like I said, you're a fine hitter, Al."

"Red," I asked him, "just tell me what it is."

"Well," he said, holding the paper up close to his face, "it figures out exactly at .36802."

"Red," I said, "I quit."

It was just that easy, for me at least. Red spluttered and argued, and I was a little taken aback myself when we got back to Muncie and I went over to watch a Wednesday afternoon game with Cedar Rapids and Red wouldn't let me in the player's entrance but made me go around through the main gate and buy a ticket. I was about the only paying customer in the stands. He started to make some noise about my contract too, until he found out that it had been a good three years since I'd had anything more formal than a letter announcing my salary for the season. In spite of how angry he was, he still wanted to keep me on. I guess he thought I was at least some sort of stabilizing force on the team, good for the rookies going up and the veterans coming down. The team, for that matter, didn't seem to do much different with or without me, and the farmer was already beginning to learn something about easing off on that wild swing of his.

What now? you may ask. Well, I don't know. In a way I've jumped back a dozen years or so to where I was standing with a B.A. in one hand, an M.A. in the other, five years of semipro ball in my bones, and a little voice in my head saying, What do you want? What do you want? I didn't know, then I knew, then I got it, now I don't know again. I only know that I didn't just quit while I was ahead, unless you consider .00002 ahead. I know I got exactly what I peddled myself for. Who doesn't, as long as he's willing to go all the way with it? And I know I didn't get much else besides. Who does? I don't know what else I know.

Footnotes to a Theory
of Place

i

Many years ago I swore I would never be a participant in an academic fiction, and yet here I am, all the same, a voting member of the Committee on Committees. So much for oaths. For what I want to ask myself is, what am I doing here? What? In the silence that follows, I am moved to start out from this point (precisely at the opposite end of the table from the chairman, and at the furthest corner of the room from the doorway) in several directions at once, but where would I go? As an old friend of mine used to say, "Which of us, if he received a telegram reading FLEE ALL IS DISCOVERED, would not pack up and be on his way at once?" Not me, that's who. I don't want to go anywhere at all.

For a long time, I pondered this curious phenomenon of my immobility in the stillness of my office, where even the cigar smoke hung motionless in the stale air. On the other side of the door, of course, my colleagues scurried away with briefcase in one hand and baggage in the other to regional conferences in nearby cities, national meetings in New York or San Francisco, international congresses in London or Vienna, Fulbrights, Fords, Rockefellers, Guggenheims, all those great names that give scholars wings. Then one day the door opened. I must have given a startled little jump; I had been seated at my desk reading Gide. It was only a student turning in a late paper, but there was something in the way he said, as he poked his head into the room, "Aha, I knew I'd find you in there," that made it difficult for me to go back to my book. The phone rang, the chairman of the department calling to say goodbye, he was off to the Folger, the Library of Congress, the annual meeting of the

100

Modern Language Association. Somewhere. They knew him in all those places. And suddenly I recognized the source of my own inertia: What sense was there in fleeing, when whatever was discovered about one was already known everywhere? I need someone to address all this to.

Let us hypothesize, then, a small man, dressed primarily in browns, who is on his way to deliver a lecture before the annual spring meeting of a literary and philanthropical society in a large American city. Fairly large. He didn't really want to go. On the other hand, he didn't really not want to go, in spite of his wife's amused response. It is the first time he has even been *invited* anywhere to do anything remotely connected with his profession. In spite of her relentless teasing, he has excused himself from classroom and committee and accepted. And she, having likewise excused herself from office and patients, is now sleeping soundly in the window seat next to him, having fallen asleep before the plane left the runway.

He, on the other hand, is wide awake, contemplating a well-before-lunch bourbon which, when it arrives, will be placed next to the stack of note cards on the little metal tray in front of him, and thinking about the future. He has been asked to lecture on "The Literature of the Midwest." That is what prompted his wife's hilarity. But when the bourbon arrives, the future he holds in his mind contains such non-midwesterners as Conrad, Borges, Nabokov, and Robbe-Grillet. And the note cards, which he flips slowly between sips at his drink, are sparsely populated and say such things as:

only three dimensions: space, time, and presence

and

*in some cultures it has always been the custom to
put something alive—a potted plant, a goat, a
child—into the foundation or walls of every new
structure (not a principle to be taken lightly)*

and

the discovery of a new word for

and

"in a first-rate work of Fiction the real clash is

*not between the characters but between the author
and the world"*

+and

in the structure of art not this ⌒

but this 〜〜〜

= the ripples of real time

and

*the earthbound ethics of airplanes: landing the
sole good*

and

*back to school in a narrative suit of olive drab
time*

and also

stay loose, swing level, and follow through

He thinks that even for committee meetings he has generally been better prepared than this.

He also thinks people would be surprised if they were aware, as he presumes he is, having recently read something on the subject in a national news magazine, of the vast numbers of travelers who change flights at the last minute, in the hope of frustrating death. Not to go by car, for the accident rate there is higher still, but only to take a later plane. Perhaps they want to be able to say to their friends, "Remember that American Airlines jet that crashed on the approach to O'Hare last fall, killing everyone aboard? Well, I was supposed to be on that plane, but I had a sudden premonition . . . " Perhaps they really do have premonitions, really don't want to die. Perhaps they believe that no matter how ill-prepared you are, if you just keep shuffling the cards something safe will turn up.

Except for the river running through it, he recognizes nothing of the city on the approach, though once he lived there for eight years. Below him, it is white, still snow-covered. He pockets his cards and folds the tray into the back of the seat in front of him. His wife shuffles about in her seat, half-waking. The plane touches down. The runway flashes by, the motors roar, I wish they wouldn't do that.

He is in the center of his hotel room, between the bed and the TV set, squatting naked before a pile of scrambled note cards, when it is pointed out to him how much he looks like some pale, scrawny savage praying for divine ignition of his wretched pile of kindling. Spare me, darling, that's not a kind thing to say to a man whose frail spark of intellect has been damped out by a hopeless subject, a sleepless night, an airplane, and an afternoon nap. I was going to leap out of bed and head for the shower, but didn't. You got there first. We should have stayed in bed and made love.

He shuffles the cards together, taps them into a thin, neat pile, looks for a pocket to stow them in, then places them on the night table, and prepares to make himself presentable for an appearance in the lobby at 6:30 sharp. Even committee work is better than this. He is appalled to uncover such a thought in his mind, like someone else's note card slipped into his pack. A title in red ink: The Real-Life Drama of Public Appearance. This, he suddenly realizes, is what I meant by an academic fiction.

Nonetheless, though a fiction should be more pliable, more amenable to his desires, both he and his wife descend, at 6:25, to a lobby where they are met by a distinguished member of the foundation. In an equally distinguished vehicle, a fawn-colored Mercedes, with the foundation member at the wheel, they rise effortlessly up the hills from downtown into the residential area. A new form of flight, he considers: he is seriously considering flight. He holds his note cards in his hands, on his lap. He had hoped to have a last chance to look through them in search of something useful, on this drive, but what with the early dark of the season, the idle conversation between his wife and the foundation member, and the major distractions of his own mind—already in rapid flight—he can see that this was a futile notion. The card on the top, which he can just manage to make out from the intermittent glow of streetlights, reads: *I've learned that the most important thing for an actor is honesty. And when you learn how to fake that, you're in.* A quote from a TV star, but as he can no longer remember the star's name, he gives up on it and looks out the window.

They are moving through streets that are, to his surprise, only vaguely familiar to him, where all the trees are elms. It is, he presumes, their integrity they demonstrate, standing up as they do, black and leafless, through the interminable winters of this latitude, out of the grimy snowdrifts banked against them, staunch and motionless. Perhaps hundreds of miles to the south, where a truer spring is underway, the elm bark beetles, carriers of the deadly and incurable dutch elm disease, are already on the march against them. So much for integrity. The University Club looms up ahead, at a bend in the street, surrounded by the tallest elms of all. The Mercedes swings sharply into its circular drive. The note cards go sliding onto the floor.

Never before has he attempted to lecture on such a full stomach. He has always been careful not to schedule his classes for the hour right after lunch, while the very idea of a luncheon committee meeting has always been enough to ruin his appetite, thereby leaving him the lone lightly fed, clear-headed member among his soporific colleagues. That has been extremely helpful at times. He also regrets the vulnerability of his position at the head of the table, actually at the bottom of an expansive U-shaped arrangement. He remembers a former undergraduate classmate, a German exchange student, who once told him how his uncle, a low-ranking member of the World War II high command, had gone hungry at many of Hitler's banquets, because though he sat well down the table, and was therefore served first, no one was permitted to touch his food until Hitler, who, as host, was served last, had begun to eat, so that by the time Hitler was lifting the first spoonful of soup to his mouth, the waiters at the lower end of the table, in order to have the next course laid out by the time the Fuehrer was ready for it, were already clearing away the now cold, but still full, bowls of soup from in front of all those hungry uncles. A little avuncular hunger is just what he thinks he needs at the moment.

During the course of a lengthy introduction, which appears to be less concerned with him than with the occasion upon which he is to speak, some sort of noteworthy local literary date whose precise nature he has missed—most likely, he supposes, the birthday of the only important writer ever to have emerged from this region—he sits with bowed head, shuffling the deck of note cards on the table before him and eyeing, fondly, the cigar container, still sealed, that lies beside his coffee cup. Between the heavy sweet dessert and that thick rich coffee, he has been called aside by a tall grey-haired gentleman, none other than the secretary of the foundation, who has proffered that expensive cigar and, as he accepted it, also passed him an envelope, sealed and demure. Slipping the envelope into his inside jacket pocket as he returned to his seat, he has laid the cigar gently on the table, planning on giving it the attention it clearly deserves when the inevitable question and answer period arrives, and he finds himself in need of something to fill the gap between the question and the answer. And there, for all I know, it may be lying still, unless some sneaky busboy made off with it, in the midst of the confusion, and tried to smoke it in the pantry, too fast of course, and so had to go out and stand coatless and shivering in the snow beside the garbage cans, taking in deep breaths of painfully cold air until the dizziness passed.

He presumes, quite reasonably, that he could get away with reciting passages from his book, for it is not likely that anybody in this room, aside from the director of the foundation, to whom he sent a complimentary copy when it was published several years ago, since it was a small research grant from the foundation that helped initiate the project, has even seen it. All he would have to do would be to toss in the names of a few midwestern novelists to accompany those—mostly continental—with whom the book had dealt. But it is futile to think that he could recall any complete passages from a book written that long ago, not read again since it was in the proof stage. He is not even certain that he can explain, without actually going back into the text to dredge up the very words he had used— and then forgotten—just what it was he had been trying to say there. A sense of where, in what, a character was, in modern fiction, and where, into what, he was going. What does that mean? Who is midwestern, anyway? Everybody? Or is that only a flighty fiction of his own recent reading experience? And what has he been doing all these weeks when, instead of looking over the same old random collection of note cards, in search of something, perhaps their true order (unshuffled at last!), or any design that might have proved useful to him this evening, he could have been putting together something sensible to say. Adding a few more note cards, is all he can remember doing. And what do they have to do with what he is doing here? Nothing, so far as he can remember, rising.

While beginning in upon what a pleasure it is, to speak to this gathered body of patrons of the arts, he cuts, without looking, his stack of note cards, lying on the table in front of him, in the middle, placing the bottom half on top. Now, looking down, he sees both the unopened cigar container which, aside from his empty coffee cup and recently refilled water glass, is all that remains of the meal, and the new top card, which reads: *the curiously ignored fact of the self-ingestion of certain mammalian organs once their purely formal function has been completed*

He remembers writing that on his last birthday, recalls that his next is now not far off, wonders just what sort of annual container he is in, and stumbles into and out of a clumsy sentence on the sense, that is, the essence, of belonging, in modern literature. Belonging-ness-in-the-context-given: a German word for it. He notes, in passing, that the Midwest is only a very small part of a much larger organism, the whole of modern literature. But somehow that fails to come out the way it was intended. Faces bent over coffee cups arch upward to look at him. Great white exhalations of cigar smoke billow upward. He shuffles his note cards rapidly as he plunges ahead. O modern literature, where are you? I mean, who is in there, wherever you are? says the voice of this native midwesterner. Or rather, how is it, that one is in there, in the midst of whatever it is? What a world! In it, or in one like it, looks grow more querulous around the table, necks and backs more arched and strained, coffee cups move about with greater frequency, until a pause is achieved.

Look, he tries to explain, in the gap that has been opened up

just for explanation, the Midwest, to tell the truth, is not exactly my—
he fishes around for a comforting sort of expression—cup of tea, he
says, disappointed. I am not even sure there is such a subject as the
Midwest. I mean, of course, the literature of the Midwest. He looks
over at his wife, midway down the left arm of the U, and sees, to his
surprise, that she has a solemn, almost adoring expression on her
face. Either that, he adds, haltingly, or there is no other subject except
the Midwest. No, that can't be real; underneath she is either chuck-
ling at these verbal absurdities or about to give way into total hilarity
at the absurdity of the entire situation. It's all the same. The real academic fiction, he is in the process of discovering, is right where he
lives. Is. When it comes to that, he says, I am a committee of one.
Then, not having meant to report that discovery aloud, he adds
lamely, so far as the Midwest is concerned. That does it.

iv

He has been, so to speak, in another country, thanks to the miracle
of communication, in its many forms. He has had a phone call (to
determine his interest in a speaking engagement, in that city of previous residency, where he was not, in a small way, totally unknown),
a letter (on fine embossed stationery, comprising a formal invitation),
and, not least, a telegram (confirmation of date, time, arrangements). He has also had a round-trip plane flight, not alone. So far
as he can remember, that was the only real telegram he has ever received. He does not presume to expect any further communication
(a note of thanks), from the same source, by any means. He does
not assume he ought to let today's, now yesterday's, activities creep
into the conversation of tomorrow's, now today's, lunch, at the Fac-
ulty Club. Much is discovered, perhaps, but much more is already
known. He is not even sure that the check, which sits now on his
dresser top, weighted down by a lovely, fist-sized hunk of polished
agate, is still cashable. But it is.

Now it is his wife who is naked in the middle of the room, sitting
cross-legged in the center of their double bed. Not a scrawny savage
at all, but more like his solid idol, breasts and belly a little overripe

and the smile on her face, whatever else it may mean, the same one that usually accompanies her yoga breathing exercises. At this hour of the night! For, of course, it was quite a late flight that they caught in that flight of their own which carried them swiftly beyond any possibility of staying overnight in that city, in that modern hotel room so carefully reserved for them. So that it was well past midnight when they arrived in a more familiar airport, and now, in their bedroom, it is a good bit later yet, though neither of them feels much like sleeping. And why should they rush to sleep. He has, come to think of it, already canceled his classes, she her patients, for tomorrow. Today. Now, perhaps, is the time to make up for the time that they slept away in that useless hotel room. He turns from where he is standing by the dresser and looks at her there on the bed, breath held deep and full, chest expanded, raised, then, with the long, slow exhalation, breasts easing downward, and says to her, "All is discovered."

More is known; that's the truth. And yet here we are. Sooner or later the telegram arrives. Almost before the word is out one is in flight, probably from an academic fiction. Midway between bed and closet you pause to reread it. This time your gaze includes the signature. "*I* sent this?" you exclaim, dropping the empty suitcase to the floor. What a question! But only on such a flightless and unmusical note as that can we, at last, turn out the lights and climb into bed together, comfortably.

Your Story

"But she derived from the eighteenth
century. She was all right."
Virginia Woolf, *Mrs. Dalloway*

I lie in bed possessed of the secrets of the human heart: a long, sad,
complex, joyous, creative, and self-destructive configuration, full of
love and care and pain and loss, balanced between an unchangeable
past and a tenuous future—at the worst, a Russian novel, and at best
. . . hmmmm, what do I do with all of this? Do I abandon an hour's
worth of fixed gazing at the spot on the ceiling where last summer I
leapt up naked to smash an already blood-stuffed mosquito, to rise
up once again, from wrinkled sheets and sodden, heavy blankets, in
dirty flannel pajamas, to try to do something with it? Rise up and use
all my abilities to make the world, as they say, "more responsive to
human needs"? That much I can do even without moving; look: the
cool sheets are the latest permanently pressed fabric, the blanket
light but warm, the still-crisp lavendar pajamas only freshly put on
last night. What could be easier? A world of my own making. The
spot on the ceiling was only a speck on my glasses, easily wiped
away with a corner of the sheet. First time in my life I've ever slept
with my glasses on—I wonder how that came to be?—though in my
dreams I've always had perfect vision. How *did* it come about that I
slept with my glasses on? In dreams, anyway, one knows how to see,
but here, in the morning, shades up, sun sparkling through the frost
etchings on the window, who knows how to do? One always wants
to get the best of everything in, but will love melt the snow on the
front walk? joy get the frozen old Ford started? happiness pay the

bills or a splendid vista to the future fix the leaky plumbing in the kitchen? What's in my heart? The secrets of the heart, that's what. Not just old experiences or the changeable present or that tenuous, oh so tenuous, future—in which it seems possible I may somehow end up going go bed with my glasses on every night—but everything, everything. Unspeakable, yes, but in an entirely new sense of the word. Those were my dreams, this is my bed, my pajamas, my flesh, my glasses—though I wonder who put them on me, in the night—but this is, of course, everybody's day. I've got to get up. There's much to be done. I swing my feet out from under the blanket and sit on the edge of the bed, wondering how I'll manage. I consider the new lavendar pajamas, which I have never worn before, and the glasses already on my face, and suddenly realize where I am. I am in your story.

In your story, he got up quickly, surprised to find his glasses already on his face, dressed, went about his morning business, ate breakfast—he rarely eats breakfast but in your story he eats quite heartily: juice, eggs, toast, butter and marmalade, tea—all very efficiently. In your life, things do not usually happen very efficiently, but in your story you will have them so. By the second paragraph he was already in the car, a Chevrolet, no, a Buick, what is a story if you can't improve things just a bit. Just a bit, however; a Mercedes would perhaps be carrying things too far, though that might well have been the car of his own choice, had this been his story. Rubbing his beard with the back of his hand, he moves rapidly with the flow of freeway traffic, a smooth and confident driver when his mind is on the road. Almost immediately the downtown exits are before him. Is he to leave the freeway here or continue on toward some other exit? His mind must be made up quickly; many accidents are caused by the indecisiveness of drivers at exit ramps. What is to be done now with this man who awakened, only moments ago, in your very hands as it were, "possessed of the secrets of the human heart"?

You are more than ready to acknowledge the primacy of such inner concerns. In your story, after all, the search for love is—if not finally *the* theme—certainly a persistent theme. You seek it anywhere and everywhere it might be found, and because it's your story you are free to carry out this quest in perfect safety. Which is not to say that you are not nervous about it. After all, even in your story, how can you know for certain whether it will succeed—or, if it does succeed, what the results of such success might be. Because your story is a real story, it has a future, into which you cannot see very far, just as it has a past, a real past, written down in the black and white of your imagination. Still, to be nervous in such a quest is at least not to subject yourself to the dangers of a similar quest in the world outside your story. Out there, there are people who might take your quest all wrong. Everything they would see, they would see through their eyes, not yours. Everything that happens would be quickly swallowed up by the powerful magic of the realm where they, not you, rule. As the hand which you reach out in order to offer a caress crosses the border into their kingdom, it changes into a claw. In their world it is no longer yours, to do as you want it to do. Their world is not the same as the world of your story, though it is not entirely different either. Contiguous. Yes, I believe they are contiguous. Your world. Their world. And I am the border between the two.

Almost against your wishes, it seems, I insist on becoming the chief character in this story, even though it is your story. The character that is I exerts itself, extruding (mostly in silence) a presence that must be felt. Often, however, I feel that I am alone in the garden and the rest of the characters are still in the house. They intend to come out into the garden—indeed, you have invited them for the express purpose of bringing them into the garden—but they have not done so yet. The french doors leading into the garden are still closed. The guests, indoors, have become quite listless. The lines they speak, slowly, to one another, or to the party at large, become spaced farther and farther apart. Like the lines they speak, like unwatered flowers, their heads droop. They become drowsy. Meanwhile, in the garden, it has begun to rain.

Can I, without an effort so great as to be totally beyond me, manage to turn your story into my story? Very doubtful. We must all work with what is given, and what is given here is, first of all, the fact that this is your story.

Question: Is that all that's given?

My Answer: By no means. There's the past, the future, more or less; there's a multitude of others, all given; there's even a possibility of other stories of the present. But that's the main given, and all others must acknowledge its preeminence. Do I, in this context, have any other choice?

Your Answer: (Your answer is longer and far more complex.)

The further back your story goes into the past, the more complicated it becomes—and for what reason? It was never a past you wanted to have for keeps, only a past you wanted to explore. Is it, then, so necessary for you to be obsessed with reading and rereading what you have written, back there when you were only beginning to learn how to write your story? So you sit at your desk with the eraser end of your pencil propped against your chin thinking, Cram it, cram the past, who needs it; I'll just go on with this thing from where I am. Doubtless you will, since it's your story. Meanwhile, the clatter of the typewriter is awaited, as is the mailman, who's at least an hour behind schedule—you keep peeking out the window to catch sight of his little blue and white truck—and though I am, of course, here, I don't know how much help I can be. My presence is well established by now, I presume, but it's your story, and you'll do what you have to with it.

This question remains, however: is it, or is it not, necessary to wipe away yesterday's dust before today's dust falls? Against us, the housekeepers, the world wages an endless and dirty war. Even in your story it must be so; otherwise the story would not be real, and your stories are nothing if not real. Dust seeps, unmentioned in the text but, of course, everywhere, between the sentences, among the words. Since I'm here I can't help being interested in how you will deal with it. I suspect you will find plot autonomous and above it all, punctuation at best an inconsistent cleansing agent, characters recalcitrant—was it, after all, for such menial tasks that you originally gathered them together?—and the proliferation of furniture, books, tea sets, wall hangings, framed photos, rubber plants—dust collectors all—a veritable betrayal. Your story is not an easy one. You would not have it so.

In your story then, life—that perennial dust-collector—is not a Greek tragedy but, perhaps, an English one. The difference is more than just one of tone. An English tragedy, you decide, is not anything to be found in the works of the Brontës or Hardy or George Eliot, all of which have something terribly Greek about them. No, you know much better than to be taken in by a bit of artificial Wessex turf. In a truly English tragedy, as in a painting by Juan Glido, the entire world—or at least all the inhabitants therein—will be turned upside down. Perhaps something to be found in a biography then, a biography of the Restoration period, say, in which a beautiful and talented woman, who has had many lovers, suddenly falls head over heels in love with . . . whom? An obscure but not entirely untalented court poet? A visiting Danish beauty, the rave of the current season? The King of the Elves? The point of this sort of tragedy is that the house doesn't burn down, no one is kidnapped or murdered, the city isn't beseiged by plague, mystery absents itself entirely. The world goes on as usual, trees and building foundations still rooted firmly in the earth. How is one to go about upside down in such a context as this?

The advantage of things being cut loose in such a fashion is, of course, a certain freedom. Think, for example, of how easily one can deal with such a practical matter as the car, of which there are so many possible versions. In your story you can make at least this one thing very simple: whenever the car appears, I am in it, continually headed south, on the freeway, the correct exit ramp guiding me easily off, in the next sentence, toward you. But in a different version, in her story perhaps, the car never leaves the garage, while in my story, if there is such a thing, the car rushes continually out of the garage and back into it, a sliding, gliding motion that goes on and on and on, that makes haste slowly, as in a dream, forward at its own pace though I have the accelerator pressed to the floor, then backward, gliding, gliding—did *I* put it into reverse?—and I tramp on the brake to no avail. The disadvantages are equally obvious.

Meanwhile, however, you are free to sleep, to work, to visit foreign museums, cure headaches without aspirin, lounge on the beaches, adjusting the weather to suit your mood, to turn the car about in the middle of the freeway, removing all police from the vicinity as you make the U-turn you've always wanted to make across the grassy median strip, and head north for a short holiday. Here now, I didn't even know you were driving.

The only problem is that once you set these things in motion, in real and active motion, they become harder and harder to control . You have lain in bed, the early sunlight filtering through your drawn shades, wondering if it's truly time for sleep to be over yet, the blue blanket kicked down around your ankles, trying to feel your way with your whole body—which is prone now, neither upright nor upside down—into the inner secrets of your story. In a moment you will rise, put on your glasses, visit the bathroom, begin to prepare your usual breakfast—juice, eggs, toast, butter and marmalade, tea—but now, like the good driver you are, keeping your eyes on the highway as the blue car speeds north, you want things to be just right. That's complicated, of course; it means, for example, that you have to take your eyes off the road to check and see if your passenger is comfortable. In your story you take on an enormous amount of responsibility. But you *do* want things to be just right. Which means that they have to be well inhabited, that they have to be seen in certain ways, that they have to work out properly. And all that while cut loose, as you have already indicated, adrift among such immovable solids as the grimy past, the rough borders of contiguous worlds, the limited imaginations of your own recalcitrant characters. Fortunately, in this story you are young and strong. You get up. Up. You are ready for a vacation. You're a good driver, good at directions, too. You're ready to take your place as a main character in your story.

How does such readiness affect me, as chief personage to date? Can I take it, you wonder, I who arose at the beginning mystified to find my glasses already on, I who succumbed to such a munificent breakfast, I who was left speeding toward an exit ramp not of my own choosing, I who found myself so suddenly a passenger in my own vehicle, all direction reversed? You stride purposefully through the room full of nearly motionless guests, not the least perturbed that they fail to lift their eyes to see you in your new mauve gown that flows, as the traditional mirror scene has already shown you, in such a fine, sensuous line from neck to floor. If anything, their heads droop lower still, their eyelids near to closing. They remain upright only by virtue of being propped up against walls, pianos, door jambs, each other. Sherry glasses and cigarettes seem about to drop from their dangling fingers; already you can see, in passing, the dust that has begun to collect in the folds of dresses, on the shoulders of suit jackets, on the backs of limp hands. Only for a moment, watching a cigarette ash break off and drift slowly floorward, do you hesitate, glancing quickly around at these dormant wraiths, wondering what your responsibility truly is. Then you step on through their midst, cross the room, fling open the french doors, peer outward into the garden, where it is still raining. I am carefully arranged against the far wall of the garden, standing on my head, a feat I have never before been able to accomplish. My feet hover inches from the stone wall, which I have no doubt used to maneuver into this unusual position. My glasses are nearly opaque with raindrops. My jacket and hat lie neatly across the edge of the marble birdbath, which is slowly filling with rain water. Because of the deepening gloom of the evening, the small pond filled with murky water that lies between us in the center of the garden, the steadily falling rain, the grey stone of the wall which serves as my background, it appears to you, standing in the open doorway, that I am suspended upside down, adrift in the twilight in the garden with my feet pointed at the darkening sky. "That's right," you say, as you pull the doors softly shut behind you and step out into the garden and the rain, "that's just right." Behind you I can see, even from my upside-down position, how the characters in the still well-lit room have begun to fade, once you've turned your back upon them. Perhaps it's only a trick of my rain-smeared glasses, but even their wine glasses seem more solid, less translucent, than they do now. You pause at the edge of the pond, feeling slightly dizzy, looking down at the rippling water, up at the rainy skies, or is it the other way around? You're good at the dark, you believe, and truly in love with the water, but still, you think, this is a little too gloomy, I imagine I want that vacation after all.

Where, in that north you have bent yourself towards, there is a cabin, there are trees also, woods in fact, a lake. Once you put an effort into imagining something of this sort, it begins to take on a proper density. The woods become a truly northern forest, tall conifers moving ever so slightly—"majestically"—in the wind, clumps of birch scattered whitely among them. The lake assumes a certain size and shape, acquires an inlet and an outlet, swampy bays in several corners where the pike lurk unseen, produces a sudden small island, perhaps useful for a picnic, over against the far shore, just across from the cabin, from which—who would have expected it already?— come the sounds of people moving about. Almost immediately, one of them emerges onto the deck overlooking the lake, a young blond woman who, though the temperature is a good ten degrees too cool for comfortable swimming, wears a skimpy two-piece green bathing suit and trails an enormous blue towel from her left hand. She is not only true but exceedingly well imagined. As she begins to descend the steep flight of wooden steps leading down the face of the cliff from the cabin to the dock, a frantic hubbub—not a single articulate word of which can be distinguished—arises from inside the cabin. She pauses on the stairs, half turning, swinging the blue towel impatiently—now it can be seen that it's not actually a towel but a wide cape made of terrycloth toweling—hears the noise following her, continues her descent, pauses again when she reaches the dock. It's clear there are too many people in there. The wind drops and the tall balsams stop swaying. The rippled surface of the lake smooths out. Blond hair lies motionless over her untanned shoulders. The cabin falls silent. Better, eh? Now at last a single voice calls out, muffled because it is coming from inside the cabin. She turns, looks back up over her shoulder, can't see anything of course. To hear better? She shrugs her shoulders, lets the blue cape drop onto the dock. The wind springs up again. Trees sway. Ripples sweep quickly across the surface of the lake. It's really too cold for swimming, especially with that breeze blowing. The voice calls out from inside the cabin again, still muffled, its edges tangled up a bit in the wind as well now. She looks back up again, shrugs again, slips quickly out of the two pieces of her green suit, lets them fall at her feet, steps to the edge of the dock and immediately dives in, her white ass flashing coolly in the sunlight. Just as she strikes the water, the screen door slams shut behind the man who emerges on the deck, leaving an empty cabin behind him and, though he knows damn well it's too cool for swimming and the water in this northern lake, especially this early in the season, is colder than he can usually stand anyway, wearing nothing except his glasses, carrying a white beach towel in his one hand and a soap dish in the other. Will he really plunge in there with you? Ah well, just look how much you've already accomplished in such a short time.

You glance back up at "her white ass flashing coolly in the sunlight" and wonder: Do you really want *that* in your story? Is it, as they say, really *you*? But who else would it be? And besides, it strikes such a nice note for finishing on—bright, cool, free, happy, sensual. . . . Why not? After all, it's your story, and look how far you've gotten along in it, toward being where you want to be. Only there is one more thing you have to do.

　Frankly, you have a hell of a time getting him in. He resists the cold in the usual determined fashion with which he confronts anything. Even though he has laid his glasses, towel, and soapdish carefully at the bottom of the steps, before walking out onto the dock, now he just stands there at the edge, and there doesn't seem to be much you can do about it. You stare and stare at the blank white page, with no apparent success, just as you used to sit and stare at the clear white skin of your arms and legs, your shoulders and stomach, when, in earlier years, you sat out in your backyard in a two-piece bathing suit of another color during the first warm days of summer, waiting for the sun to turn you brown but not seeing anything happen. Finally, with a great shrug of impatience, you jump to your feet, walk to the edge, and, with the full force of your body, which is almost exactly as tall as his, simply push him in. He enters the cold, cold water with hardly a splash. Bone-chilling, is what it occurs to you he must be experiencing, and you wonder, as you wait for him to surface, if you should write that down. You know he is a good swimmer, and that he particularly delights in swimming great distances underwater, slipping up on other swimmers unseen, but you also know how he feels about the cold. You cannot see him. The water is pure but dark, the deep amber darkness of the mineral and algae rich waters of this northern lake country. Its coldness feels good to you, but you know he fears getting cramps in his legs. Needless to say, you will not give him any cramps in your story—it's not your purpose to cause pain— but if he gets them, you'll be there to help. You'll sink down into the dark waters after him, knowing that the sunlight and everything else you have created is back up there above you and thinking, like a woman from the age of candles and high winds, I can do this, I'm good at the dark.

And that's good, you conclude, because there's so much of it.

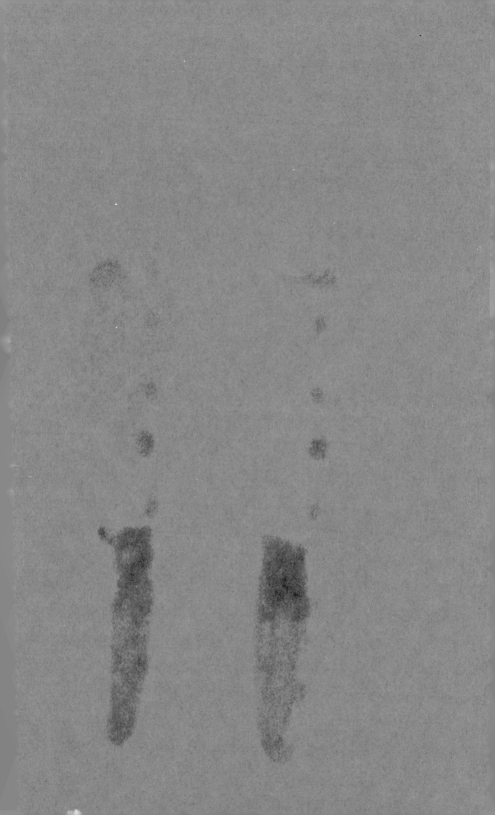